ABOUT THE AUTHOR

M. L. Tompsett is an emerging author of action paranormal fantasy romance. She has been creating worlds to escape to since she was a little girl. Years later, she is still enjoying her writing in her imaginative make-believe worlds with interesting characters. Finally, moving forward to the big, wide, scary world of digital and print publishing.

Married to her childhood sweetheart, they live in Victoria, Australia and have two fully grown extremely talented sons.

With her books, out in both ebook and in print - softcover - she is excited to see something she has been working on for far too long finally become a reality.

Drop by and check her out on her website and blog or social media

www.mltompsett.com

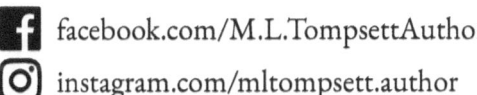

facebook.com/M.L.TompsettAuthor

instagram.com/mltompsett.author

ALSO BY M. L. TOMPSETT

SHIFTER ROMANCE AND URBAN FANTASY

Kept in the Dark of Love and Lust

Kept in the Dark of Lies and Deceit - book two

PARANORMAL FANTASY

Sex, Lies And Family Secrets - Series

The Guy Next Door - Book one

Dark Surprises - Book two

You Never Know - Book three

It's You - Book four

What You Know - Book five

Vampire book

Her Vampire Fated Mate

Contemporary Romance

SECOND CHANCE AT LOVE - SERIES

Insta Bride

The Bodyguard's Convenient Marriage

Ghost of a Chance in Love

Secret Heiress

Kept in the Dark
of Love and Lust

M. L. Tompsett

Tompsett Publishing ™

Book One: **Kept in the Dark of Love and Lust**
By M. L. Tompsett
Copyright © 2019 by M. L. Tompsett
ISBN 978-0-9953858-8-7
eBook: ISBN: 978-0-6482507-9-1

Cover art designed by **Tompsett Publishing**™ Cover images licensed via Adobe Stock.

Published in Victoria, Australia by **Tompsett Publishing**™ 2019. This book in the series, 2ND edition published by **Tompsett Publishing**™ & **M. L. Tompsett Author**™ **2026.**

* **Disclaimer:** This book is a work of fiction. All characters in this book have no existence outside the imagination of the author and have no relation to anyone bearing the same name or names. Any resemblance to actual individual persons, living or dead, or actual events is purely coincidental. Characters, businesses, places, events and incidents are either the products of the author's imagination or used in a fictitious manner.

* **This** book contains coarse language, adult themes, blood, shifters, young love, violence, nudity, handsome - muscled men. Intended for readers 18 years and older. This book is written and edited in Australian/UK English. Which means spelling will be different.

DEDICATION

For my Family always!

To my boys, thank you for allowing me to type and create, including driving you all mad with the world of paranormal fantasy, and all things in the world of romance – love you guys.

P.S. *- Heads up. Sorry, there will always be more.*

Never allow someone to dictate, 'you can never do something you enjoy.' You can do anything you put your mind to and create a world you believe in.
A world to escape and have all types of fun in!

BLURB

Hard working city girl, Misty Statesly travels to a coastal town in Victoria to save her job from sabotage and hopefully win over her new clients from a sleazy work colleague.

The feeling of déjà vu fills Misty when she runs into a gorgeous guy in the town's supermarket, and it happens again when she meets her new client – Braven O'Geary.

Braven is mesmerised by the mark on the inside of Misty's thigh when they find themselves in a compromising position. A matching mark he had given his soulmate whom he was led to believe had died in a car accident with her parents, some sixteen years earlier.

Can Braven and Misty outwit the cat shifter clan and survive the evil plot his ex-fiancé and the alpha have orchestrated? Will Misty regain her lost childhood memories, and fight for the man she loves, embracing her new strange world or will she die this time for real?

Kept in the Dark
of Love and Lust

A voice so close and yet so far away.
The sensation of knowing, and not knowing at all.
A love so young ripped apart.
Is death an end or is it only the beginning.
Never take love for granted, for it might be gone tomorrow.

— *M. L. Tompsett*

PROLOGUE

Sixteen years earlier

BRAVEN O'GEARY HOLDS HER TIGHT, HIS SMALL ARMS wrapped around a girl who fits against him like she has always belonged there. Malisty Ashton. His soulmate. His little mate. The one his instincts cling to with a fierceness far too big for his ten-year-old body.

He shouldn't feel this way — he knows that. They're too young. The adults whisper about bonds and timing and rules he doesn't fully understand. But something inside him is pushing, urging, warning. Must complete the mate bond. Something is coming. Something bad. And every instinct he has screams at him to keep Malisty close.

She sits on his lap, tiny legs folded around him, her little arms looped around his shoulders. Her soft snow-white hair brushes his chin as she tucks her face beneath it, trusting him completely. The swirl of her blue-green eyes still dances behind his eyelids.

He squeezes her gently, gathering courage he doesn't feel. He needs to say this right. Needs her to understand. Needs her to choose him.

"Malisty," he says, lifting his chin like he's trying to look older than he is, "you're my soulmate. I'm yours. We'll be together forever." His voice wavers. His heart doesn't. "You do want to be my soulmate... don't you?" His eyes search hers, pleading. "You feel our bond?"

Malisty bites her bottom lip, thinking hard in the way only a five-year-old can — earnest, serious, adorable. She presses a tiny hand to her chest, right over her heart.

"I feel it," she whispers. "Right here."

Her eyes shine up at him, trusting, glowing with something far too big for her small frame.

"I want to be your mate forever. As long as Mumma doesn't tell me off."

Braven almost laughs — almost — but the urgency inside him won't let him. He glances around the empty room, making sure no adults are near. If they're caught, they'll be separated. He can feel time slipping away.

Malisty shifts on his lap, trying to get comfortable, and Braven freezes. Something in his body reacts to her nearness — something he doesn't understand — and panic flickers across his face. He tightens his grip on her hips, keeping her still, not wanting to scare her, not wanting to ruin this moment.

She looks up at him, eyes wide and full of trust. And then something in her softens, settles. She knows. Somehow, she knows.

"Braven," she whispers, "I love you." His breath catches. "Bite me." Her little voice trembles, but her eyes don't. They glow with certainty, with the bond humming between them, with the kind of love only soulmates can share — pure, instinctive, unbreakable.

Braven's heart swells until it hurts. He cups her cheek with a shaking hand.

"I love you too, Malisty," he whispers back. "You're my soulmate. We'll be together forever. No one will ever separate us again."

And in that moment — two children, too young to understand the consequences, too bound to stop — their fate seals itself.

Two Weeks Later
Jazey & Janelle

A SINGLE WARM TEAR SLIPS DOWN JAZEY ASHTON'S cheek before he even realises it's fallen. He stands beside his daughter's bed, watching her tiny chest rise and fall in soft, even breaths. Malisty sleeps curled on her side, one small hand tucked beneath her cheek, her snow-white hair fanned across the pillow like spilled moonlight.

His heart fractures all over again. The pain is sharp, deep, a tearing ache that spreads through his ribs and settles like a stone in his gut. He wipes his face with the back of his hand, but the ache doesn't ease. It only grows.

Malisty's lips twitch into a small, dreamy smile. Her long lashes flutter once, twice, before settling again against her flushed cheeks. She looks so peaceful. So innocent. So unaware of the storm gathering around her.

Jazey's knees nearly buckle.

His daughter's life is in danger. All of their lives are. And the proof of it — the damning, undeniable proof — rustles in Janelle's trembling hand behind him.

The test results. The ones he prayed would never arrive. If only the doctor had never run the bloodwork. If only the prophecy had stayed buried. If only their little girl were ordinary.

But she isn't. She never has been.

If things had stayed simple, Malisty would have grown up beside her acknowledged soulmate, Braven O'Geary — the pack leader's eldest son. The boy who adored her. The boy she adored. Her sixth birthday is only weeks away, the first of many ceremonies meant to strengthen their bond.

But Xavier changed everything. Xavier, the little black wolf pup from the neighbouring wolf pack, who followed Malisty everywhere. Xavier, who loved her with the same fierce devotion Braven did. Xavier, who should never have been able to bond with a panther child.

Two soulmates. From two different clans. Two different species. Impossible. Forbidden. Dangerous.

Jazey remembers the moment he found them — three small children huddled together, pinky fingers bleeding, the faint scent of a forming bond in the air. Malisty's tiny hands stained with both boys' blood. Braven and Xavier marked by her in return.

He'd frozen. Shocked. Terrified. And he'd told no one but Janelle. And then two weeks ago, everything shattered.

Janelle had found Malisty on the playroom floor, whimpering, bleeding, Braven crouched over her with a fresh mating bite on his neck. The scent of a completed bond hung thick in the air. Braven's parents had stormed in, ripping their son away from Malisty's trembling body, causing the jagged bite on her shoulder. The second bite already on the inside of her thigh.

Too young. Too vulnerable. Too bound. To know what they had done. But done nonetheless.

Jazey hears Janelle's voice behind him, soft and shaking. He turns, stepping quietly from Malisty's room.

"Jazey... we have to do something." Janelle's eyes glisten as she clutches the papers to her chest. "These results prove it. Our little girl is the one from the prophecy. When she hits puberty, she'll be able to shift into either a panther or a wolf. At will."

Her breath shudders. "Just like the prophecy said. The first of her kind. And the clans will call her an abomination. They'll kill her, Jazey. They'll kill her before she ever gets a chance to live. And then they'll come for us."

He pulls her into his arms, holding her tight as she trembles. He's already made his decision. Already started the preparations. Already accepted the cost.

"You're right," he whispers into her hair. "We have to leave. The clan must believe we died. It's the only way to keep her safe." He left off the — to keep us all safe.

Janelle glances at her watch — and pales.

"Shit. The O'Gearys will be here in thirty minutes. What do we do? What are we going to do?"

Jazey cups her face, steadying her. "We pack everything away. We act normal. Today might be the last time Malisty and Braven see each other until fate brings them back together. And I believe it will. I feel it in my soul."

He swallows hard.

"I just pray their bond isn't strong enough to destroy them when we take her away."

He presses a kiss to Janelle's forehead.

"We leave in two days."

CHAPTER ONE
MISTY

PRESENT DAY

TRAFFIC ROARS PAST MY PARKED HOLDEN SEDAN, each passing truck sending a shudder through the chassis. Brilliant. Exactly what I need — a vibrating car, a blaring indicator, and the nasal whine of the office idiot screeching through my speakers.

Why did I answer the phone?

Why did I pull over?

Why am I like this?

I rub my forehead, exhausted and starving after hundreds of miles on the road. My GPS glows cheerfully at me — ten minutes until Lakes Entrance. Ten minutes until I can collapse into my accommodation for the next eight days. Ten minutes until peace.

But no. Of course not. Because the universe hates me.

The moment I saw the office number flash on my screen, I knew I had to take the call. I should've let it go to voicemail. I should've trusted my instincts. But no — I answered.

And now I'm stuck listening to him.

Kenté. Wannabe Boss. Human migraine.

His snivelling voice grates through the speakers, setting my teeth on edge.

"Misty, when will you be arriving in Lakes Entrance? The meeting for tomorrow needs to be confirmed."

My forehead scrunches. What is this chirping little gremlin up to now? My meeting is already arranged. Confirmed. Double-checked. Triple-checked.

"Kenté, why are you calling me? Everything is organised."

He barrels over my words — typical. "Misty, you're about to meet one of our biggest Victorian clients. I don't want you to stuff up the account. I don't know why Samuel is letting you handle this. I have more experience—"

I tune him out before my brain melts. This man is digging his own grave with every syllable. I hit record on my phone the moment I heard his voice — I've learned the hard way.

A pair of birds swoop overhead, carefree and dancing through the sky. Lucky bastards. I wish I could fly away too.

"Misty," he continues, "I've emailed you the new contracts. The ones you drew up were inadequate. Silly mistakes like yours cost the company millions. You're lucky I caught them."

My breath freezes. Is this idiot for real?

Then he drops the bomb. "Oh, and I've already emailed the new contracts to the client in Lakes Entrance."

Dark spots flicker at the edges of my vision.

No.

No, no, no.

I cut him off mid-rant. "Kenté, you're breaking up. I can't
— hear — you — are you — reception must be bad in this area.
I have missed ...said, can you... Kenté, I'll repeat. Can you...me?
Are yo..."

I hang up before I say something that gets me fired. I stop
the recording, duplicate the file, and email it to myself and LJ.
Insurance for me. I've learned, always keep proof when dealing
with snivelling deceitful jerks.

I need a friendly voice. I tap LJ's picture on my screen. She
answers on the third ring, warm and familiar. "Hey, Misty!
How's the drive?" Her tone rises and with a laugh says, "Are
you there yet?"

Relief washes over me. The old joke. The comfort. The
normalcy.

"LJ, hey. I'm not interrupting, am I?"

"Misty, don't be silly. What's wrong? Something's
happened." Her tone back to serious friend mode. How does
she do that? Psychic. Has to be.

I stare at the blinking indicator, listening to its relentless
tick-tick-tick as three massive trucks thunder past, shaking
my car.

"Um... I just got off the phone," I mutter.

"Oh no. Let me guess. Idiot Kenté strikes again?" This girl
knows me too well.

"Yeah. He sabotaged another account." My voice cracks
with frustration. "This is the final straw. I have all the proof
now. When I get back, I'm filing an official complaint. He's

done. He just emailed his contracts to my Lakes Entrance clients. He's stuffed up big time."

"Oh, Misty..." LJ sighs. "I hope he's fired soon. He's already cost you two clients this year. Surely your boss can see what Wannabe Boss is doing."

I shake my head. "My boss gave me another warning on Monday. Me. Not him."

My throat tightens. Tears prick. I hate this. I hate that he's dragging my career down with him.

"I'm sorry, LJ. I'm just... annoyed. And tired. And done."

"Hey," she says gently, "you have nothing to apologise for. He's jealous. You're one of the youngest corporate leaders in sales they've ever had. He can't stand it."

I breathe out slowly. She's right. She always is.

"Thanks, LJ. I need to call my client and start damage control. I'll talk to you tomorrow. Love you."

"Love you too, my little kitty girl. Drive safe."

I smile despite myself. LJ has called me that ever since she saw my tattoo — the black panther with blue eyes, the wolf with green eyes, the tree and water scene. She loves it. I... tolerate the nickname.

I don't tell her the truth — that the tattoo covers scars from an "animal attack" I don't remember. That my parents dodged every question I ever asked.

I end the call and scroll through my contacts.

Something inside me urges me to hurry. A strange pressure. A whisper. A presence I've felt since childhood — the one my parents rushed me to a specialist for. The one that vanished for years, only to return as a quiet voice in the back of my mind.

A voice that feels... familiar. I shake it off and tap the name on my screen.

BRAVEN O'GEARY

Time for damage control. Time to save my job. Time to call the man who has no idea how much chaos is about to hit both our lives.

Chapter Two
Misty

I stare at the name glowing on my touch screen.

BRAVEN O'GEARY

The letters tug at something deep inside me — a whisper, a brush of familiarity, like a memory hiding behind a locked door. I frown. I shouldn't know this name. Not personally. Not from anywhere except his file.

But the whisper lingers.

I shake it off. He's just my client's son. My contact. A man I've never met, never seen, never spoken to. No photo. No social media. Just a neat little bio that says he's five years older than me, rising fast in the family business, and likely to take over from his father.

Professional. Straightforward. Easy.

Hopefully.

I pick up my phone again, my finger hovering over his

number. My stomach tightens. I need to fix this mess before Wannabe Boss tanks my entire career.

Deep breath in.

Tap.

The call screen flashes, and the ringing fills my car through the speakers. My shoulders tense. My spine straightens. My brain starts running through every possible scenario — from polite professionalism to full-blown disaster.

The ringing continues. My pulse climbs. I wonder what his voice sounds like. Smooth? Sharp? Old? Young? Arrogant? Bored? Gods, please don't let him sound like Kenté.

"Hello?"

I jump.

Oops. Someone answered.

Focus, Misty. Don't crap your pants.

I inhale quickly. "Hello, I'm trying to contact Braven O'Geary. Can you assist me at all?"

Brilliant. Who else would answer his phone?

"Yes, this is Braven O'Geary. What do you need assistance with, Miss?"

Oh.

Oh, his voice is... nice.

Deep. Warm. Confident.

Maybe a little too sexy for my current level of professionalism.

"Hi, is it okay to call you Braven?"

"It depends on who you might be, Miss. Have we met before, perhaps?" His tone dips into a teasing lilt.

Great. A flirt. Just what I need.

"Okay, Mr O'Geary, this is Misty Statesly. We arranged a

meeting two weeks ago through your secretary. I'm from Smithton, Brown and Hamminway. I'm on my way to Lakes Entrance to meet with you regarding your family's financials. My employer has handled your portfolios for over twenty years."

Silence.

A long one.

My stomach twists.

Then— "Okay. I was under the impression I was dealing with a man named..." Papers rustle. "Ah. Kenté Braigs. He phoned me this morning and sent new contracts."

My jaw drops.

Wannabe Boss strikes again.

"Excuse me, Braven — Mr O'Geary. I know Kenté Braigs. He works in my office. But your family's portfolios have nothing to do with him. I've been handling them for three weeks. May I ask what he said?"

"He... I..." Braven hesitates. "I was disappointed, actually. He sounded like he knew nothing. I nearly called your company to say we'd be taking our business elsewhere."

Oh gods.

Oh no.

Damage control mode: activated.

"I'm so sorry you had to deal with that, Mr O'Geary. I don't know what game he's playing, but I'm the one assigned to your accounts. I'd really appreciate the chance to meet and sort this out. I've reviewed all your portfolios, and there are a few things I'd like to bring to your attention."

"What do you mean, things out of place? What other portfolios?" His voice sharpens.

"Are you still available for our meeting tomorrow morning? Or would you prefer to meet in two hours? I can come to you, or you can come to me. I think it's best if you see everything I've prepared."

A pause.

A long, evaluating one.

"Miss Statesly, my gut is telling me to give you a chance. But after that phone call with Kenté Braigs, I'm not sure your company is competent."

Fantastic.

Time to kiss arse.

"Mr O'Geary, I'm truly sorry. This isn't the first time he's interfered. I've been documenting everything for the CEO so I don't lose my job. I'm not making excuses — I just want the chance to show you the correct portfolios and recommendations. If you can come to me, I'll order dinner. My shout."

Another pause. Then—

"Oh really? And what kind of dinner were you thinking of wearing?"

I blink.

Did he just—

Dinner I'll be wearing?

Grrrr.

Flirt alert.

"Mr O'Geary, I'm glad to hear you have a sense of humour. But to clarify — I'm not wearing tonight's meal. Unless we're in a relationship I don't know about, food will not be involved in our business proceedings."

A laugh rumbles through the speakers.

A deep, warm, sinful sound.

And just like that, heat curls low in my belly.

Moist.

Tingly.

Fantastic. My professionalism is dying a slow death.

"Okay, Miss Stately," he says, voice shifting back to business. "I'll meet with you. You may have saved your company for now. Where and when?"

We talk for a couple more minutes, settling on meeting at my temporary apartment first, then dinner afterward. We say our goodbyes.

I check the time.

Two hours.

Two hours until Braven O'Geary shows up at my door.

I pull back onto the road, crank up my music, and let the beat fill the car. My mood lifts. My shoulders loosen. I even start singing.

Maybe — just maybe — I've saved my job.

CHAPTER THREE
MISTY

WITH THE GPS ANNOUNCING I'M MINUTES FROM Lakes Entrance, relief loosens something tight in my chest. The big blue welcome signs appear, and I exhale like I've been holding my breath for hours.

A bend in the road, then another — and suddenly the world opens up.

"Wow... what a view."

The ocean stretches out in front of me, glittering under the late-afternoon sun. Fishing boats bob in the distance, tiny silhouettes against the water. I drag my eyes back to the road, but the scenery keeps tugging at me — the sharp turns revealing more ocean, more sky, more of the lakes that give this place its name.

A massive boat catches my attention. A long pipe juts from its side, blasting brownish sand into the air.

A dredger. I read about it — clearing the inlet so the fishing boats don't get stuck. Seeing it in person is... weirdly impressive.

This place is beautiful. Peaceful. A boating lover's dream. And after the day I've had, I'll take any scrap of peace I can get.

I cross the main bridge, slow at the roundabout, and spot my accommodation ahead — water on my right, the tall building on my left.

Can't miss it.

I pull into one of the allocated parking spots and climb out of the car. My legs protest immediately. Hours of driving will do that. I stretch, arms overhead, neck cracking, eyes drifting up the multi-storey building with its balconies overlooking the water.

Not bad.

Not bad at all.

I think back to my earlier meetings — Inverloch at 11:30 a.m., Cowes at 8:00 a.m. Breakfast, coffee, pastries, clients, contracts. A whole day of coastal towns and business smiles. And now here I am, in sunny Lakes Entrance, a fishing village with dolphins, water sports, and hopefully fewer idiots than my office.

I grab my handbag, check for my phone and booking documents, lock the car, and breathe in the salty air. It tastes like freedom. Or maybe exhaustion. Hard to tell.

Reception is quick. Ten minutes later, I'm back in my car with a keycard and a map.

And a surprise. A two-bedroom apartment. I booked a one-bedroom. Reception insists someone from my work changed it this morning.

Fantastic.

Wannabe Boss strikes again!

I drive into the undercover car park, find a spot, and haul

my bags toward the entry. The doors are locked — of course they are — but the keycard works. I juggle my luggage, hit the elevator button, and ride up to the fifth floor.

The hallway lights flick on as I step out. Sensor lights. Fancy.

I follow the signs — right, then left — until I reach my room. A shiver crawls up my spine, a memory flashing of the last time work booked accommodation for me. The filthy room. The used condoms. The dirty laundry. The way I marched straight back to reception and demanded a new room. I still want to shower every time I think about it. I swipe the keycard. The light turns green. The lock clicks.

I push the door open with my shoulder. And stop.

"Oh... wow."

Sunlight floods the open living space. The kitchen, dining area, and lounge blend together in a clean, modern layout. A huge flat-screen TV hangs on the wall. The bedrooms sit at opposite ends of the apartment.

But it's the wall of glass that steals my breath.

Floor-to-ceiling windows. A massive balcony. And beyond it — the lakes, the ocean, the sky. This place is stunning. Romantic, even. Pity I'm here alone.

I step onto the balcony and look down at the pools — the indoor heated one with glass walls, the outdoor lagoon-style one with umbrellas and sun chairs. The view is ridiculous. I lean against the railing, inhaling the sea air.

"Well, Misty, you can't stand here all day. You've got work to do. And probably some arse-kissing." I roll my eyes at myself and head back inside.

The balcony has a table, four chairs, and an electric BBQ.

Not bad. If I have time later, I might sit out here with a drink and pretend I'm on holiday.

I explore the apartment quickly and claim the master bedroom. King-size bed. Plasma TV. Two padded armchairs by the window. A walk-through wardrobe leading to a huge ensuite with a deep bath.

Yes.

This is exactly what I need after today.

I lay out my business suit on the bed for the meeting. Freshen up in the bathroom. Change into jeans and a casual top. Unpack. Set my briefcase on the kitchen counter.

The wall clock tells me I've got just enough time to hit the supermarket, grab supplies, come back, shower, change, and be ready before Braven arrives.

Wine for me. Beer for him — just in case.

Before I leave, I pull out my phone. Time to text Mr Braven O'Geary my floor and room number.

And hope to the gods he's as professional in person as he sounded on the phone.

CHAPTER FOUR
BRAVEN

I END THE CALL, AND FOR A MOMENT I JUST SIT THERE, staring at my phone like it's bewitched. My pulse is still thudding in my ears. My body is wired. My instincts are pacing under my skin like a caged animal.

Who is this woman?

Whoever Miss Statesly is, her voice alone hits me like a punch to the gut. Smooth. Warm. Confident. And something else — something that coils low in my stomach and refuses to let go.

I drag a hand over my face, trying to steady myself. My body reacts to her voice in a way I haven't felt in years — not since I was a boy and my soulmate was still alive. The memory of Malisty's name flickers through me, sharp enough to sting.

My gaze drops to my hand. The faint pale line on my ring finger stares back at me — the ghost of the engagement ring I wore for Liasa. The reminder is like cold water thrown over my head.

Liasa.

My mood sours instantly.

Nine days ago, she was my fiancée. Nine days ago, she was planning our future. And nine days ago, she was also in my bed with my own brother. I saw it. Heard it. Smelled it. The betrayal still burns.

I shake my head hard, clearing the memory. No point dwelling on it. Liasa wanted children. I couldn't give her that — or so we thought. And she didn't love me. Not really. She loved the idea of power. Of status. Of being mated to the future clan leader.

But she never had my heart.

Not truly.

That part of me died with Malisty.

Or so I believed.

Until Miss Statesly's voice slid through the phone and something inside me — something ancient and buried — snapped awake.

I lean back in my chair, exhaling slowly. "Get a grip, Braven."

But my mind betrays me, conjuring images of a woman I've never seen — Miss Professional, Miss Sexy Voice — and imagining her beneath me, warm and willing, her breath catching as—

My phone vibrates violently on the desk.

I jump.

Damn it. I really need to focus.

Marcus' name flashes across the screen. Perfect. Just what I need — my idiot brother calling at the worst possible time.

I answer with a clipped, "Braven O'Geary."

"Braven, why do you answer the phone like that? My name shows up on your screen."

I bite my lip hard enough to sting. It keeps me from saying something I'll regret.

"Marcus, is there a reason for your call? I have a business meeting to prepare for."

"Business meeting? I thought it was tomorrow?"

I close my eyes. Either Marcus is losing brain cells, or he's been talking to that parasite Kenté. Neither option surprises me.

My phone buzzes again — a text. I glance down.

Miss Statesly.

Her floor and room number.

A slow smile spreads across my face before I can stop it. My chest tightens with something sharp and electric.

Miss Sexy Voice.

I force myself back to Marcus. "Marcus, I'm busy. What do you want?"

"I... wanted to talk to you about something. Something you should know."

"What is it? Are you okay?"

"I'm fine. It's Liasa. No one's heard from her since she moved out."

I grit my teeth. "Marcus, Liasa and I are done. I won't be getting back with her. She was sleeping with someone else."

Silence. Then a gulp I hear even through the phone.

"What do you mean she was sleeping with someone else?"

"I saw it. With my own eyes."

"Oh... shit. Braven, I'm sorry. I really liked Liasa."

"Maybe you should get with her then," I say, the sarcasm sharp enough to cut.

"What? Why would I—"

"Marcus," I interrupt, "I know you slept with her. In my bed. On my lounge. You don't hide something like that from a shifter."

Another gulp. "Braven... I didn't mean to. She was upset. I tried to comfort her and one thing led to—"

"Marcus." My voice drops, low and cold. "You don't sleep with your brother's fiancée. Ever. I need space. Stay away from me for a while."

"I'm sorry, Braven. I'll do anything to make it up to you."

"For your own wellbeing, give me time. And if she's pregnant — man up. Because it's not mine."

I hang up before he can respond.

The silence that follows is thick. Heavy. But I push it aside. I don't have time for this. Not now.

I check my watch.

Forty minutes until I meet Miss Statesly.

Forty minutes until I see the woman whose voice has my instincts prowling.

I grab my suit jacket, keys, phone, and briefcase. I'm halfway to the door when something hits me — a strange, sharp sensation that ripples through my chest.

I freeze.

Close my eyes.

Focus.

There it is again — a tug, urgent and primal, pulling me toward something. Toward someone.

My eyes snap open.

"Misty."
The name slips out before I can stop it.
Something's wrong.
I can feel it.
Like a warning.
Like a threat.
Like my soulmate is in danger.
And I need to get to her.
Now.

CHAPTER FIVE
MISTY

WITH THE DIRECTIONS FROM RECEPTION, IT DOES not take me long to drive to the local supermarket, off Church Street. Quickly making my way along the aisles with my shopping trolley, I select different items required for my eight-day stay. Eight whole days, away from the *Wannabe Boss* and the hustle and bustle of the city.

First, on my mental list — I begin to collect, the cold items — fresh milk, yoghurt, some frozen ice creams, butter, eggs, and some bacon, followed by a couple of bottles of lemonade and orange juice.

In the lolly aisle, I pick up a couple of different packets of lollies and chocolates. I soon discover the microwave popcorn in single bags and decide I need to chill out tonight and sit back with a big bowl of popcorn and a good movie or two after my meeting with Braven.

I quickly find the DVD display, and promptly look over the DVD selections. I pick the first DVD off the shelf and read the back of the case before placing it in my trolley, to add to my growing DVD home collection. As I went to reach for the second one, my body bumps into something hard. Somehow, my hand managed to grip the DVD box and lift up the plastic case when my brain catches up, and I realise, I have just bumped into someone.

Oh, Gods, there are tingling sensations through my hand from the contact with this mystery person. My nose quickly picking up this person's after-shave or is it deodorant? Whatever it is, this person is definitely a man, a man who smells good, good enough to lick, mmm. My tongue is instantly licking my lips, with erotic images of licking this mystery man from head to toe and everywhere in between. Hmmm. Nice.

A husky voice breaks my erotic thoughts and daydream, "Sorry miss, did I hurt you? Congratulations, by the way, you managed to grab the last movie in the sequel." Hmm, nice voice, a very sexy sounding voice.

My tongue continues to lick my lips in a sensual movement. My eyes are slowly taking in the man beside me, his manly scent, making my brain go to mush. Who is this man? His body, so enticing and built, mmmm.

His legs look strong enough to hold a girl up against any hard vertical surface, while he erotically thrusts into her hard and with her legs wrapped sensually around his narrow waist enjoying every powerful thrust. Hmm-mmm and look at his chest and shoulders, they seem to be well built as well. If I didn't know better, I would think I have developed a disability with drooling.

Oh yeah, this guy is sex on a stick. My eyes continue until I see his left hand and notice a wedding band, sitting on his finger. I feel my brain literally hit the brakes on the sensually erotic thoughts. *Oh, damn it, he's married. That's about right; they usually say all the good ones are either taken or gay.* I glance up to his face. *Oh, Gods, this guy is gorgeous, why did he have to be married?*

Ah, shit, why is he looking at me funny? Uh-oh, I think he is talking to me, and I have failed to reply, well failed to listen more like it.

Oops. It's not my fault; mister sex-on-a-stick is sexy as sin and super gorgeous. If I had the time, I would continue to stand here and look at him and daydream. A girl can dream — can't she?

I start to smile and find he is taller than I first realised, tilting my head back just to look up at his handsome face. Oh, boy, this man is tall, what height would he be? Hmm, he would have to be at least six foot two, maybe three. I slowly come back to my senses, and I think my time being rude is finished. Now, what had he been saying to me?

"Um, hi, sorry, no I am not hurt, and I have not seen this movie yet. I love the other ones in this series, and I have been waiting for this one to be released on DVD."

Oh, Gods, I'm making a fool of myself. I look back at his handsome face and then it hits me — his eyes. There is something about his eyes. It is as if I know his eyes from somewhere. His sexy emerald green eyes, but from where? I do not remember his face at all.

Before I can stop it, I unknowingly make contact with the stranger's hand. Our hands make skin-to-skin contact, setting off a whirlpool of sensations through my now tingling body.

Oh wow, what is going on? This is just so strange; it is as if the stranger is somehow connected to me.

That female voice I swear I hear every so often in my head starts to make noise, hearing her say, '*uh-oh*' - while hiding deeper within my mind, making herself as small as possible.

What in the world is happening? Why would the imaginary voice in my head decide now of all times to hide? What is she hiding from?

With a quick intake of breath, I quickly pull my hand away from this sexy stranger. I make myself stand a little taller and glance at his handsome face. "Um I know this sounds like a pick-up line, I promise I'm not trying to pick you up or anything. I have already noticed your wedding band, so I know you're married, but it's just your eyes, they seem so familiar to me, but I do not know from where."

The sexy guy with his dreamy green eyes keeps looking at me funny; his eyes seemed to be searching mine for something when his lips start to move.

"No, I don't think we have met, because I would never forget such a beautiful face like yours." My face is instantly heating from embarrassment, just great, this is all I need, to walk around looking red-faced and embarrassed.

"You have one fortunate wife; she must be one powerful woman."

A frown appears on the sexy man's face. "Why do you say that?"

I start to giggle. This stranger has me acting like a hormonal teenager with a huge crush. "Sorry, it's just that you're so good looking, your wife would most likely be fighting all sorts of women off with a stick, to keep them away from you and your bed."

His eyes opened wide with shock. "Geez lady you sure are forward — however, thanks for the compliment. My beautiful wife does not fight any women off. It seems my charm only works on you. Pity you weren't around a few years ago, I think my wife would have had her hands busy trying to keep me to herself." I begin to blush again. Just great, this guy will have me beetroot red before I leave the store.

"Um thanks, but a few years ago, my schooling had taken up all my time... Sorry." My bottom lip pouts, and my shoulders shrug before I shyly smile.

The sexy guy started to grin at me again, causing my body to behave in a manner it never has before so that any minute now I will be a puddle here on the floor. Oh Gods, what is this guy doing to me? I have not felt this way before with any other man, but how? He is married for God's sake. I should not be feeling like this.

"Um look, I have to go. I have a few more things to purchase. I had better let you go so you can get back to your fortunate wife, um before she attacks me with a big stick." His smile, more prominent now, showing off his straight white teeth. I wonder if he knows he is making me wet. I just hope I do not smell. I need to get out of here. Now.

"Bye, enjoy a different movie." I smiled back at him over my shoulder and walk away with my DVD still in my hand. Knowing each time I watch this movie, I will picture this guy's face. Oh well, at least I got to see a gorgeous hunk of a man.

It is not long before I have managed to select the different items I require for my stay. I even grab a box of condoms for a laugh. LJ would love them, a box of different colours, textures and styles, including several extra-large sized condoms. I wonder if they have the sexy male to fit into the condoms around here. If that other guy back there is anything to go by, I might just find myself getting lucky. Yeah, I don't think so.

I quickly pay for my items at the checkout and remind myself to head next door for the bottle-shop. It does not take me long to walk into the liquor department and purchase a couple of bottles of wine and a six-pack of Australian beer.

I glance down at my watch and notice I only have thirty minutes until Braven will be arriving for our meeting. Oh bugger, I had better get moving.

CHAPTER SIX
MISTY

As I WALK BACK TOWARDS MY CAR WITH ALL MY purchases, a strange sensation comes over me as if something is not quite right. Casually looking around, I glance around the carpark and my surroundings. Once I am sure no one is following me, I glance towards my car, confirming it is still in its same parking spot.

With the strange feeling becoming stronger, urging me to walk a little faster, even though I cannot see anything or anyone out of place, unease still fills me.

I start to look down towards the ground once again when the hair on the back of my neck starts to rise. Instantly I know something is wrong, even before I notice the dirty shoes.

A pair of dirty work boots fill my field vision, less than three metres in front of me. I glance to my left and then to my right to see who else is around before I let my eyes take in the dirty, scruffy man with the dirty shoes — who is still standing in front of me — waiting.

Instead of acknowledging him, I attempt to walk around him, not wanting to be robbed by this guy or attacked. Relief quickly fills me knowing I keep my car keys and phone in my pocket, when shopping and not in my handbag. Just in case someone comes up and takes off with my bag.

I manage to keep the scruffy man in my field of vision at all times, only for him to move in the same direction with each step I take. The annoying man keeps his body in front of mine, not allowing me to pass. Oh great, I do not have time for this, and I do not want any trouble.

"Excuse me, Miss, can you spare me a few dollars?" The tone of his voice sets the hair on the back of my neck to stand straight up, whilst weird vibes start hitting my body with full force.

Dirty scruffy man's voice does not match his filthy appearance. From a rough guess, I would say he is just over six foot, wearing a long dirty trench coat over — is he wearing black leather pants? Yep, they sure are, leather pants and some kind of dark pullover jumper. This guy is definitely not homeless.

I glance up towards his face, his dark shortish hair swept down, covering strong cheekbones, dark facial hair covers the lower half of his face, but it's his eyes, a piercing blue colour. His eyes are far too bright and focused on me. I know this guy is not some man to palm off; this guy is trouble, trouble with a capital T. Lucky for me I had taken the self-defence classes this year, just in case anything like this ever should happen.

My heart speeds up; as I'm reminding myself, I have to remain calm. I quickly glance around us to see if this person has any friends, sure enough, two other men come out from between parked vehicles and slowly approach me, from two different directions.

Oh, damn. I fight the urge to turn and run. It does not take a genius to work out; I am in trouble and running would do me no good.

I glance first at the big and dumb looking guy on my right, with a short buzz cut of dirty blond hair and a scar on his face. He looks like he has more fat than muscle on his body. I would call him Numb Nuts.

The second guy on my left, is a scrawny looking little shit, with long greying stringy hair and a long grey beard, his clothes covered in mud and filth, making it look like he sleeps on the streets.

The sound of laughing was coming from the two men, causing my heart to beat a little faster. Now I know I am in trouble. With too many thoughts flying through my head, I try to focus and remember my self-defence lessons. I have to keep these guys in my sight and not allow them to get behind me or circle me.

I don't know what it is, but I am getting strange overwhelming vibes from these three. Something is very different about them. If I were reading one of my paranormal fantasy books — the protagonist would start to think these three males were not human. Lucky for me, I live in the real world full of humans.

My stress and fear levels increase. I have to say something, anything, to learn what these idiots really want.

"Gentlemen, what do you think you are doing and don't give me the beggars crap. I would advise you to walk away now and go harass someone else." Hoping I sound brave and like someone who didn't give a crap and most of all, not looking scared shitless.

"Look, lady, we can smell your fear. All we want is your bag and your car and to take you for a little drive. We can all have some fun while we are at it. Got it?" The dirty, scruffy man said with a big mocking grin on his face, showing his straight white teeth. His friends laugh again in an annoying mocking tone.

I try to build up some inner courage and keep all three in my sight. "Look bud, you and your friends just leave right now, and there will not be any trouble, but touch me, and you are the ones who are going to be hurt." Great, what am I doing encouraging them to attack?

"Are you trying to scare yourself, lady or me? Because I do not feel scared, not as you do, I can see it and smell it. It's very intoxicating." The dirty, scruffy man said, in a mocking voice. Lifting his head to the air and sniffing the air then licking his lips. Great, what is he a dog or something, he can smell it? Geez, they are weird around here.

Before I can take a deep breath to reply, all three men come at me at once. Somehow my body begins to respond automatically — I quickly release my shopping trolley.

First I dodge the scruffy guy, just as my palm of my left hand comes up into the face of the scrawny guy. With a bit of extra force to go with it, I can feel his nose give way as my hand makes contact to his face. Not a pleasant feeling to go with the sickening crunching sounds of breaking cartilage.

With my body in motion — my right foot lifts and kicks up hard and fast between numb nuts guy's legs, connecting with his tender bits. The impact hard enough for Numb Nuts guy to stop what he is about to do, falling to the ground reaching for his balls, while the scrawny guy moves his hands to his nose, attending to the blood gushing from it.

I spin in the direction of the filthy guy, ready to fight him. Only to notice he is just standing there, with a big grin on his face and starting to move his hands.

I ready myself once more when he starts clapping. This idiot is standing there — clapping. What the...? His clapping confuses for a few seconds until I snap out of it and quickly look back over at the two idiots, making sure that they are not going to attack or harass me in a hurry, and then I look back at the filthy guy.

"Take your friends and leave me alone, or do I need to phone for an ambulance for you all?" I demand.

This person – the filthy strange man just kept on clapping at me, which is starting to piss me off and no longer feeling as scared as I had been a few minutes ago.

Filthy guy began to speak, in his arrogant tone, "Look, lady, you seem to handle yourself okay. We just wanted to see what you could do. We know what you really are, so stop pretending with us. You need to come with us now to see our boss." Was this idiot for real? Me — go with them. Ah, I don't think so. Hang on what does he mean he knows *what I am*?

I take a slow step towards my car and say, "Look Dick Wad," Yes the new name suits filthy guy, I think I shall continue to name him Dick Wad for now on, "just take a hike, and take your little friends with you. Get the fuck out of my face now, have you got it. I am not going anywhere with you. So tell your boss, if he wants to talk to me, he needs to make an appointment, just like everybody else."

I begin not to feel scared or worried anymore. Instead, I feel extremely pissed off, and by the look on his face, he knew it. He gave me a strange look and then glanced around before his eyes settled back on me.

"Lady you are making a huge mistake, by not coming with us. Some advice for free, keep away from the cat..."

What the...?

"Look you, you... You whatever you are. Do not tell me what I can and cannot do. What do you mean; you know what I really am. Last time I looked, I was a fully-grown woman. What... What cat do you mean? I do not have any cats."

The filthy guy — Dick Wad, just looked at me, his smile slowly fading off his face.

"You really do not know, do you? You do not know what you are, and what we are?"

Not allowing him to finish, I demand, "Look bud. All three of you look like filthy homeless guys, causing trouble. Me — I am only a grown woman with no pets. Now I have to go because my ice cream is melting and I have a business meeting in less than an hour."

With that, I walk over to my shopping trolley, gripping its handle tightly causing my knuckles to turn white. My heart beats triple time as I quickly walk in the direction of my car. As soon as I am close enough, I release the boot latch with the key fob. Within seconds I dump my shopping in the boot.

I try to keep my body from shaking and press the key fob several times before I finally manage to open my driver's door, getting into my car, and locking all the doors before my butt is fully seated. I fumble with my keys as I race to start the engine, place the car in gear and drive off as quickly as I can.

Wanting to feel safe, I turn the steering wheel and head back towards the only other place I know. I drive along the side road before turning onto the main strip — back to the apartment. I keep watching the rear vision mirror, only to notice all three men are gone from view.

Not sure to feel relieved or worried, but every few seconds, my eyes scan my mirrors — looking, searching, and feeling extremely scared.

Who are those men?

What did they really want with me?

CHAPTER SEVEN
MISTY

WITHIN MINUTES, I HEAR THE BACK WHEELS OF MY car spin against the road surface and my car races into the undercover park. I make sure I park my car in a well-lit area, under one of the lights.

I feel my heart racing as I scan my surroundings. Not seeing anyone around in the dimly lit car park, I try to slow my breathing down enough to prevent myself from hyperventilating.

As I exit my car, I notice my hands shake as I hit the car boot release and my knees unsteady with each step I take. I inhale another deep breath and slowly move my unsteady feet to the back of the car.

Probably freaking myself out more than I need, my eyes are constantly looking up and around.

Geez, Misty get a grip, I keep thinking to myself. Even though I continuously make sure there is no one here watching me. I realise the only sound my ears are detecting is my heart frantically racing against my ribs and my pulsing blood, drowning out any other sound in my ears.

I give my head a quick shake to clear it and reach down into the back of the car. My hands make quick work of whipping all the bags of shopping from the car boot. With a loud heavy bang, my car boot closes, glancing back around me, looking, and searching with my eyes, including the little crevice areas of darkness.

Surely, I am safe now. Did those filthy men manage to follow me? My eyes dart around again. *Geez, girl, keep this up, and you will end up in the hospital with anxiety.* I give myself a mental slap to clear my thoughts.

I have to move, and I have to get out of the car park. I can feel my body trembling with shock, and think it is time to move my butt back to my room. I manage to turn my head enough, to assess my surroundings once more until I can see the closest entry and rush towards the locked doors of the building. Luckily, I placed my keycard in my back pocket. Juggling all the shopping, I manage to pull out the keycard and gain access to the interior of the building and rush into the open elevator, hitting the button to close the door and then the floor level to my apartment.

Once I reach my floor and am safely through the door of the apartment, and in the kitchen area, my emotions overwhelm me, and I burst out crying. My bags of shopping left discarded on the kitchen benchtops. My brain is straining to play catch up of the past half hour.

What just happened to me? Why did those strange men attack me? Why me? And what did they mean? Before I can think much about it, the wall mounted phone starts to ring —

making me jump, and wondering if those filthy men have followed me after all.

Panic starts to seep back through my terrified body. Should I answer the phone? I can feel my body continue to tremble with each breath I take. I slowly start to move towards the ringing telephone, at the same time looking out the windows for anything strange.

Even though I am five floors up and cannot see the ground from where I am standing, but you never know who might jump onto the balcony. I watched Spiderman, Batman, and Superman enough times to know anything is possible with the right equipment.

Before I know it, my fingers have circled the receiver. I look down and stare at my hand, fisting the plastic receiver. Hearing someone talking I start to frown, until I realise, the voice I can hear is speaking through the phone. Oops. Feeling silly, I lift the receiver shakenly to my ear.

"Hello," Oh, Gods, even to my own ears I can hear my voice sounding cut up.

"Misty, it is Braven O'Geary. We have a meeting."

My brain slow in processing the man's words. Who? Meeting? Braven...

"Oh, um, yeah. Mr Geary, I mean O'Geary, I'll buzz you straight up," I manage in a shaking tone.

"Misty, are you okay?" I can hear the concern in Braven's voice.

Not wanting to explain my ordeal over the phone, I reach up and hit the button on the apartment phone to allow Braven O'Geary in the building and up to my floor.

Within seconds or maybe minutes, someone is knocking on

my apartment door. I kept staring at the receiver of the phone and then at the door, and then looking back to the phone. Feeling numb and maybe a little cold, until a male voice sounded from the other side of my door.

"Misty, are you there? Open the door. It's me, Braven." The knocking did not stop. "Misty, open the door please, I know you're there, you are safe now. Open the door for me please and I can help you."

Wha... what ...who? Oh, bugger Braven is at the door. Oh, man, this is not good. I think I might have gone into shock or something. I don't feel too good.

It takes me a couple of fumbled tries, to place the receiver back into its cradle and stumble towards the door.

"Hang on Braven, I...I'm coming," I screech out.

Somehow, with shaking hands, I manage to unlock the door and open it. After a few blinks of my eyes, it finally dawns on me. There is a dark figure looming over me.

Instinctively I step back and blink a few times before I close and slowly open my eyes once more. With my thoughts confused, I try to concentrate on the hugely impressive tall man standing before me, in my doorway.

With a hitch to my breath, my foggy brain begins to clear, and all my previous thoughts and confusion, disappears — gone, vanished — poof. My heartbeat slows enough to calm my erratic nerves. A strange warm sensation envelopes me, tugging me towards this stranger, encouraging my body to respond in a manner I have never felt before.

I glance down to the floor and try to clear my mind — without success. I flick my focus towards the stranger, and the only thing my brain is contemplating is the tantalising image before me.

My focus rakes down his black suit pants, cut just right, not leaving anything to my imagination. I attempt to swallow the pooling moisture in my mouth and end up gulping instead. Slowly my eyes travel upwards to a narrow trim waist and continue higher following the lines of his blue dress shirt. A tailored shirt is covering a well-toned chest with the top three buttons undone exposing tanned smooth skin underneath.

My mouth turns dry at the sight of this man, and I attempt to lick my dry lips. His shoulders are broad and look strong as if they can handle the weight of the world on them. My eyes rest upon his face, and I slowly drink in his features.

Not realising I have been holding my breath; I start to feel light-headed from lack of oxygen. I manage to take in a deep breath, and I glance back over and down his sexy body and all the way back up to his face.

First, his strong looking chin with a slight dimple in its centre, which I want to run my tongue over again and again. Nicely sculptured shaped cheekbones.

His nose, not big, but well-proportioned to his face and those eyes. Now those eyes can stop traffic and most likely make a woman wet with pleasure, from twenty paces — eyes surrounded and framed with long dark lashes. What colour are his eyes, though? Are they deep blue or green or maybe a little of both? However, these eyes seem so familiar to me as if I should know them, know — him. And his hair, his hair is dark brown not black, and short all over his head.

Yet when I look at him as far as I can tell, I have never met this man before, and still, I feel like I should know him from somewhere. I feel a bone-jarring sensation deep within me to his presence as if I know him?

I feel something deep down to my soul and sense an acknowledgement — I want to hold him and never let him go.

What is it with the gorgeous guys around here? Every time I look into their eyes, it's as if I should know them.

"Misty, can you hear me; have you heard a single word I have been saying?" What? Oh, crap, he has been talking to me, and I have been too busy eyeing his body. Well, it is a lovely body. I think I started to blink again. "Do you like what you see?" He asked with a cheeky grin.

"Yes," Oh, do not tell me I just said that aloud. Crap. By the look on Braven's face, I think I just did. Oops. "Um, yes, Braven, I have heard you." I manage to break eye contact and try not to turn the colour red, even though my face started to feel hot. "I am not feeling very well. I was attacked at the supermarket car park, off Church Street."

The smug smile fades from his gorgeous face. "What, when? Have you called the police?" Now he just sounds worried and maybe a little overprotective as his eyes roam over me. "Come, sit down. Are you hurt? Did they touch you? They didn't rape you, did they?" His concerned and worried voice, changing into authority tones with each word.

I allow Braven to walk me towards one of the dining chairs, feeling the heat of his hand on my lower back. My eyes close at the sensual feelings of his touch through my clothes, as I sit down.

Oh, Gods, it's happening again, feeling Braven's hands slide along my body until his hand is holding my arm, sending that tingling feeling, up and down my body. What is it with these men? How can two different men I don't know cause this effect on me?

"Misty, please talk to me," Braven requests.

For the first time since being back in the apartment, I look down at my hands properly. My eyes grow wide with shock and concern. "Oh, my Gods. Oh, my Gods, it's gross, I have to get it off. I have to wash the blood off." I attempt to stand up, and my knees buckle before I can lift off the seat. Braven is in my way, and I have no choice but to sit on the dining chair with his big body preventing me from standing up.

"Misty, are you hurt? Is this blood yours, or does it belong to someone else?" A little sarcastic laugh escaped my lips. My head starts to shake before I even have a chance to answer.

"No, it belongs to one of my attackers," my voice far too quiet for my own liking, it sounds like I am whispering. Still looking down at my hands, Braven lifts my hands up to his face with his strong ones. Did he just sniff; did he just smell my hands? Please tell me he did not just smell the blood, covering my hands.

"Misty, what did these men look like? Were there two or maybe three attackers?" How would Braven know how many men there were?

I answer anyway in a whispering voice, "There were three of them. The first one resembled a filthy homeless guy, but when he spoke, his voice. His voice was too strong to belong to a homeless guy; it seemed to hold power. Plus he was wearing leather pants. As for his two friends, one of them I nicknamed Numb Nuts. He was a big dopey looking guy. But in the end, he very much would have very numb nuts." I just smiled at my own joke and quietly giggled. "As for the third one, he was skinny, scrawny, and this is his blood." I glance down at my hands, seeing the blood had dried on my skin, "He should have a broken squashed nose."

Braven shifted a little in front of me. "Wow, you sound like you can take care of yourself in a tough situation. What happened to the first guy, did he touch you at all? What did he say to you?"

I look up, my eyes meeting his, now I can see; his eyes are blue and with flecks of dark green. Wow, what do you know? Nevertheless, they are gorgeous eyes. I feel like I can find myself getting lost in the depth of them. Braven blinked breaking the connection.

What was I saying?

I shake my head from side to side to clear it enough to remember.

Oh, yeah, the filthy guy. I started talking again, "That is just it, what he said to me, is the strangest thing." I shake my head at the strangeness of the whole situation.

I glance up and towards the big glass windows, and continue talking, "The filthy guy, otherwise known as Dick Wad, first asked if I could give him some money. I knew straight away when I noticed his friends that I was in trouble. I told them to go away." I turn my head and look back to Braven's face, "He said he could smell my fear. Yeah, smell. He also said he knew what I was. And that I should know what they are as well."

With a shrug of my shoulders and shake of my head, I still have no clue what the filthy guy had been speaking of? "He had me there; I just did not understand what he was getting at. I just said to him that last time I looked, I was a woman. And that he and his friends look like homeless people. But in the end, he said to me, that 'I must not know what I really am,' or 'what they are,' and 'I needed to go with him to talk to his boss.' I told him that his boss needs to make an appointment if he wants to meet with me and that I was leaving because I have a meeting," I say with another shrug of my shoulders, "the filthy guy went on to say that I *should stay away from the cat*. Whatever does that mean? I don't even have one," I say in a rush.

Braven continued to look at me and stayed quiet. He looked like he was deep in thought.

"Oh crap, my ice creams, they are probably melted by now, and the rest of my food is most likely ruined." I move my head and try to look around Braven's body for my shopping. I vaguely remember carrying the bags into the apartment. I do not remember placing anything away.

Braven slowly stood up and turned. "Misty, why don't you go and get yourself cleaned up. Maybe go and have a shower. I'll put away your shopping and see if your ice creams can be saved or not, okay."

I focus on making my body move and stand. I concentrate, hoping my knees will support me. I managed to stand slowly up, locking my knees in place and feel my legs begin to shake, but at least I am standing. I turn my head towards the noise from the plastic shopping bags, and notice Braven is already sorting and placing the grocery items on the kitchen bench.

"Um yeah, thanks, that sounds like a good idea. I'll be in the main bedroom. Just make yourself at home."

As I start to turn, Braven turned around with one of the bags of shopping. "Misty, I think you might need this bag. It has some toiletries in it which might come in...handy." I look up to his face and wonder why his voice changed a little.

The first thing I see is a big smile on his face, no, more of a cocky grin, for some reason, this cocky grin began to annoy me.

I move forward and quickly reaching for the bag of shopping, from Braven's outstretched hand, my hand managed to grab one handle of the bag, causing the bag to open wide, exposing the top contents of the shopping. OMG. Now I know what he was smiling about. Oh, Gods, how embarrassing. The box of condoms is right there on top, like a sparkling diamond.

First, I feel my face heat up from the embarrassment, quickly replaced with annoyance. With a growl, I quickly snatch the rest of the bag away from Braven, before saying in a huff, "Look, it's none of your business. Plus I always think a girl should be prepared for any situation. While here, I might or might not get a chance to use them. So can we just drop the subject, please? This is embarrassing enough as it is."

Braven laughed and tried not to smile, "Ah um you're right, a girl should never be unprepared. Please, this should not be embarrassing. It's good to see that you take precautions. It shows me that you are a very mature young woman. It is a pity a lot more girls do not do the same thing. Can I ask you a personal question? Is it more for just protection, or is it because you're not on the pill?"

Wow... What the f... "Braven, I think that is a little bit too personal, don't you think? And just for the record, I do not go around sleeping with guys wherever I travel to. And before you ask, no, I am not in any kind of relationship. I just purchased them to remind me. *Me*. That I do have a life. It does not mean that I will use them any time soon. But just to be on the safe side, it is better to be prepared. I might meet a man that I find sexually attractive, hopefully, one that is not married." My mind quickly thinks of the handsome, sexy guy from the supermarket. "While here or somewhere else. So on that humiliating note, I will go and have that very much-needed shower. If the milk did not spoil, feel free to make yourself a hot drink." With that embarrassing venture, I turned and walked quickly to my bedroom with my bag of shopping, including the box of condoms.

Chapter Eight
Braven

I TRY NOT TO FOCUS ON THE GENTLE SWAY OF MISTY'S enticing hips before they disappear from my view. As tempted as I feel to follow her, I force myself to remain here in the kitchen. It is better if I keep myself busy and focus on the bags of shopping. It does not take me long to pack everything away, and fingers crossed her ice cream will survive for another day.

Instead of following the sound of the running water and joining Misty in her bathroom, I decide I might as well make myself a cup of coffee while I wait. I focus on finding the kettle and filling it with fresh water before switching it on at the power switch.

I still do not know how I did not break the door down when I first arrived at her apartment. When I had sensed and smelt Misty's fear and traces of wolves had my heart racing. Then when Misty opened the door, and my eyes landed on the blood on her body, my beast inside wanted out, wanting to protect and fight for her. Never before have I felt so powerless. Well, not since my childhood mate —Malisty was taken away from me, all those years ago, only to be told she was dead.

Oh, my God, and when I finally touched her, my dick instantly stood to attention, nearly ripping a hole in my pants. How Misty did not see my bulge standing out at her, I do not know. The girl needs protection, not groping and sex.

The fragrance of her shampoo and soap fills the air, nearly bringing me to my knees. My fingers grip the bench top, causing my knuckles to turn white. My beast is urging me to go to the girl and mate with her.

Get a grip Braven this woman is a stranger. A business associate, a defenceless human, get a hold of yourself. There will be no sex, well no sex until all the business dealing is complete.

Just as quickly, I turn back around towards the kettle. I focus again on making myself a cup of coffee just as I pour enough milk in the mug the sound of the water in the bathroom being turned off grabs my attention. Oh, no.

Now my mind fills in the blanks with a vision of a naked wet woman several feet away from me, which causes my solid hard length to bite into my zipper. I shake my head to try to clear the erotic images, but it does not help when I can hear Misty moving about in her room. Without much thought, I pick up my cup of coffee and start walking towards her bedroom doorway, which happens to be wide open.

My eyes just about pop out of my head when I see Misty wrapped only in a bath towel. I watch her move about her bedroom until she turns towards the bed. That is when I see it. Oh wow, Misty has a large tattoo on the back of her shoulder.

I think my eyes are playing tricks on me, because, I could nearly swear, one of the tattoos is a picture of me. What in the world, why would Misty have a tattoo of a large black cat on her body. Hang on; she also has a tattoo of a large wolf. What is going on here?

CHAPTER NINE
MISTY

At last, feeling clean and refreshed after my long steaming shower, I walk back out to the bedroom with just a large white soft fluffy towel loosely wrapped around me. Moving towards my large bed, I notice I still have my suit on it.

Bugger, this is not the time to be wearing the suit, I think to myself. Picking my outfit up from the bed and heading back to the walk-through wardrobe, I hang the suit back up with my other clothing.

I stand in front of my clothes, with my bare feet sinking into the plush carpet, I glance down towards my toes. My mind wanders to different thoughts, imagining two people romantically entwined on a rug just like this one. It reminds me more of a big sheepskin rug than carpet. Giving my head a shake, I try to clear it free from the sexual images I imagined. I look back over my clothing and decide to wear something comfortable.

Once I sort out my mind, especially the horrible thoughts

and what happened today in the supermarket carpark, I realise that I really do not feel comfortable attempting a business meeting. How am I going to reschedule the business meeting with Braven? Wow. Braven. Another handsome, sexy guy to contend with. Only this one is in my apartment, metres away. One thing I did notice, he wore no ring on his left hand.

I reach for my lacy underwear, a clean t-shirt, and a fresh pair of jeans before I turn and walk back out towards my bed. Just as I place the folded clothing on the bedspread, my hand reaches for and loosens the knot holding my towel in place.

With a quick flick of the knot, my bath towel begins to slide down my toned body and bunch around my feet, allowing my body to air out and breath before I dress.

I stretch my arms high above my head first before bending forward. I try to remember to stretch before dressing; it helps to relieve the feeling of the clothing restrictive against my sensitive skin, plus to stretch out any stiff muscles.

When I hear a noise behind me, I feel my heart race, and I try to prevent the panic from overtaking me. I realise someone is in the room with me and I glance over my shoulder.

Oh, my Gods. Braven is standing there in the doorway to my room.

Even though I do not know this man, I prefer to be seeing him standing in my doorway than either one of those filthy men from the carpark.

I casually glance at his muscular-looking body leaning against the doorframe with a coffee mug engulfed in his hand. His eyes are slowly roaming over my naked body as if he was here to map every inch of my nakedness. With my wide-open eyes, I feel like I am a deer stuck in car headlights. I gulp, trying to gain some composure.

My brain is quickly trying to gather something to say, "See anything you like?" I throw Braven's words back at him from earlier, "or can I help you with something?"

I instantly stand up tall as if this kind of thing did not affect me. Yeah right. As if I have strange men in my bedroom, while naked... I manage to take in a slow breath. My eyes rove back up to Braven's face. I notice the hungry look upon his handsome features — hungry for me. Oh boy. I gulp again, fighting to push air into my lungs. I can feel the heat from Braven's hungry gaze, and for the first time, I am lost for words.

Oh, wow. This is entirely new to me; I have never received this kind of look from a male before. A first of many things...

Braven's voice interrupts my fast-moving thoughts, "Both," watching a cheeky smile form on his face. "...oh yeah, I like. You have a very nice body by the way. That is one very nice tattoo on the back of your shoulder. I would not have guessed you for someone having a tatt."

My eyes instantly follow his lips, just as a big smile forms on his face. Braven slowly licked his sensual lips while his eyes casually look me up and down again and a strange tingling sensation starts low in my belly, heading down between my legs.

I gulp again. I try to force a big breath of air into my lungs.

Oh, my. I can feel my body beginning to heat up ready to go up in flames, just from Braven's intense gaze. I watch Braven start to move as his body moves from the doorframe — walking, no, stalking towards me. Ah, what is he doing?

Uh-oh, I attempt to turn back towards the bed to place more distance between us, forgetting how close I am to the side of the bed. All I manage to do instead is to fall back on the big bed. My arms and legs are going in all directions, when my feet leave the floor, at the same time allowing Braven a full view of my very exposed naked body.

I feel extremely embarrassed and very exposed, and try to move, but before I can roll to my side, Braven is there, right in front of me, between my legs looking at my naked thighs.

"Ah, Braven, what do you think you are doing?" I begin to feel mortified. I glance from the top of his head and up to the ceiling, "You're in my bedroom, and now you're between my legs. Don't you think this is kind of moving a little too fast, for two people who have just met and not even kissed yet?" I attempt to make the situation less embarrassing.

I wait for a reply from Braven, but he did not say anything or move. I look down at the top of his head and notice Braven keeping his focus on my thighs. Well, I hope it is my legs he is looking at, but then my thighs are spread wide open.

After a few more seconds or maybe minutes, Braven slowly inches his head forward, slowly closer between my gaping thighs. With his hand, he reaches forward to touch me. Then it occurred to me. He is looking at my scar on the inside of my thigh.

I freeze, my body is held in place, just from his presence alone. His fingers are moving straight for the scar and lightly touching it, causing me to jump, but it is the feelings I am having that concerns me more.

The feelings of an electrical current, not painful, more of an erotic tingling sensation with each sweep of his touch, his touch becoming arousing. If Braven continues to touch me, I am going to become wet, and the embarrassing part is, he will see.

I can see a strange look in his eyes. Braven remains focused on the scar, while his finger continues to trace around the shape of it, over and over again, my breathing becoming faster. What is he doing to me? Whatever it is, it is feeling good.

"Misty," his voice startles me, "who gave you this scar? Tell me. Whom do you belong to? Who is your mate?"

Ah, what? Some of my senses come back to me. What is Braven talking about? I don't belong to anyone, and what is it about a... mate?

I glance back at his face, feeling my heart rate increase as I reply, "Look Braven if you are quite finished playing between my thighs. I would like to get dressed now."

Braven circles my scar once again, making me feel confused and breathless. As frustrated as I feel, he is not listening to a word I am saying. "Braven, what are you talking about? I told you, I am not seeing anyone; I am not in any relationship. So, can you remove your hand from my thigh." I leave out the part of how his touch is making me wet. I don't know why, but it feels so good. I'm going to come if he keeps touching me.

With another sweep of his hand, Braven's touch sends erotic chills throughout my body, and I feel as if I am about to, *Oh, Gods my pussy wants to explode.*

I look up at his face, to see if he has listened to a word I have just said.

"Braven, I think you have embarrassed me enough. Can I get dressed now?"

The sad truth is, my fantasy of being with a gorgeous man between my spread thighs, has come true. For some unknown reason, I do not feel threatened by Braven. My heart keeps telling me — I know this man. And yet my brain is confused and denies knowing him. But why do his eyes seem so familiar. And yet, I have the feeling I have been in this position before.

With a slight tilt of his head, Braven looked up to my pussy, and his nostrils flared, and I watch the pupils of his eyes dilate. I gulp and attempt to crab crawl backwards. Uh-oh, I think I am in trouble.

Before I can blink, Braven moved his face towards my wet lower lips, inhaling deeply. I froze into place and watch his hot wet tongue dart out between his lips and swipe up and down my slit, causing my butt to lift off the bed.

Shocked by his actions, I attempt to move only for his hands to push me back down against the bed, holding me down as his tongue lunges forward once more, licking frantically at my flesh.

With conflicting emotions, my brain is saying one thing and yet my body wants something else. My body and brain battle against one another until my body overtakes my thought process, allowing my legs to part, giving Braven even more access to my eager channel.

My brain seems to acknowledge Braven is not a threat to me, even though my thought process abandons me to his talented tongue. Before I can stop him, Braven increased his tempo feasting on my swollen wet folds, opening me wide with his hands, spreading my sensitive, swollen wet lips before his mouth.

Oh, Gods. What he is doing feels so good. Why have I denied myself — my body this type of pleasure before now? Hot erotic sensations are running from my pussy and vibrating throughout my body — from my head back down to my toes.

He knows what he is doing — between him sucking on my

clit and tonguing my needy channel an orgasm is fast approaching. This is a hell of a lot better than using my hand and my little mini vibrator.

Within seconds I feel his fingers dual with his talented mouth. Braven began pumping into me with one finger then quickly changes it to two slowly stretching me while his tongue makes quick work of my sensitive stiff clit.

Oh, Gods, my body arching up in the air then it hit me. I have to be dying an erotic death as my orgasm slams me onto the bed. My whole body is shaking and convulsing from all the pleasure Braven is giving me. He continues to use his mouth, but something is missing. With every erotic sensation, my body is going through; I know what I am missing. It is — he — Braven, is the missing piece.

"Braven, I, Gods, Braven, I need you in me now." I don't know if I was yelling, but he got the message.

I did not see him get undressed, but my eyes did take in his naked muscled body, as it covered mine. He positioned his body between my spread thighs and lifted my legs, wrapping them around his waist as he moved forward — the feeling of something big and hard at my sensitive entrance, nudging and pushing.

The sensation of my lower lips spreading and stretching, just before my brain acknowledges pain from my vagina trying to stretch and open wider is coupled with the feeling of Braven invading my trembling body. With another harder nudge forward, my body starts to stretch wider, accommodating for his big hard length. With a quick hard thrust of his hips, he manages to thrust all the way forward.

I try to move at the intrusion, but it was no use, as my eyes snap open. "Oh, Gods" there is a pain, sharp pain. As if, my body is tearing in two.

Once again, I try to move my body away from the intensity of it. Now I know I am screaming, my ears vibrating from my voice. "Ah, bloody hell that hurt. It hurts..."

But, before I can comprehend, what just happened, Braven pulls back, and then he is thrusting back into my body all the way to the hilt, my thighs being nudged as wide as they can go. In, out, in, out, in and out, his body continues to pump and thrust. With each thrust and glide of his hips, the pain starts to subside and finally begins to feel good. Without being told what I need to do, my body starts to move in motion with his.

His thrusting is becoming stronger. Harder. The pain is all but gone. The fullness is feeling even better — this feels fantastic — as my body stretches to accommodate Braven's huge length. I need Braven to go faster and push my feet into his arse cheeks.

My back arches off the bed, as my body is going up in flames with each slide and thrust of his powerful hips — now this feels like home, this experience feels so right. We are like the pieces of a broken puzzle, finally falling into place to become one.

My hands are running up and down Braven's back, feeling his muscles in motion, my fingernails scoring his back with each of his downward, forward thrusts, my breasts wobbling back and forth with the pounding of his cock. My naked, stiff pointed nipples scratch along Braven's muscled chest.

Braven increased the speed of his thrusts. He moves so fast I don't think he is even breathing, the noise of his ball sack hitting the naked moist flesh of my arse cheeks, with every thrust echoing throughout the room. I can feel another orgasm approaching, ready to burst forth.

"Oh, my Gods, oh, my Gods, Braven, oh, yeah, oh, Braven ...faster." Somehow, Braven started to thrust harder and faster, pleasure racing throughout my body again, and again.

Then it hit. My body starts to convulse and shatter into thousands of pieces of something I cannot explain. I have never had an orgasm like this before. It feels as if I have left my body while white fireworks exploded all around me. My soul feels free. Surrounded by love and protectiveness as it begins to merge with something — is that another soul. Is my soul merging with Braven's soul, as two separate entities become one?

Braven moved his head, and I just made out his mouth opening wide on my shoulder, near my neck. I feel his tongue sweeping along my skin, as he tastes me, causing my body to heat up and I am about to combust from his touch.

My head automatically moves to the side to allow him better access to my slender neck. Before I know what he is doing, Braven bites down hard on my flesh. Pain is instantly registering in my brain. My back is arching off the bed, a scream ripping out of my throat. The pain is quickly subsiding to pleasure.

With another thrust of his strong hips, an intense sensation pushing me to do the same to him — to bite him, just as he did to me. I manage to turn my head and opened my mouth wide, biting down hard on his shoulder. My teeth pierce through his hot skin, followed by his warm enriched blood flooding my mouth.

Braven started to growl in my ear, thrusting even harder

than before, plunging forward. I can feel his penis butting against my cervix; with each thrust. Pleasure and pain erupt with each thrust of his hips.

After a few more, powerful thrusts of his strong hips, I can feel something else happening. The sensations are becoming overwhelming, an overload of mixed emotions bombarding me, exploding inside my head, but most of all, I can see Braven smiling at me in my mind. How in the world is he in my head like this? How can I hear his voice, hang on, his voice and face are in my head?

'*My mate, I have found you.*'

Just as everything starts to fade, my brain registers that word again... MATE.

Then nothing.

CHAPTER TEN
BRAVEN

WHAT IN THE HELL, JUST HAPPENED?

My mind is racing with the knowledge, I have just mated with this stranger. If I did not know any better, I would say this woman is my mate, my beautiful little soulmate — Malisty.

But how can that be? My Malisty is dead. She was killed along with her parents in a car accident, some sixteen years ago.

However, that mark on her thigh, it is so much like the mating mark I had given Malisty all those years ago. And it is definitely a mating bite mark.

Ah, shit. I must be squashing Misty, with my weight on her delectable body. Damn, I think she has passed out.

Just as I start to pull out, it finally registers in my sex-hazed brain. My dick has partially shifted. I feel the spiked head scrape the inside of Misty's virginal body. Oh, Gods, no. Oh, shit. I instantly stop moving. But it is too late.

Without knowing what I had been doing, that part of my

body has shifted to my cat form, enough to mate with Misty, and most likely set off her heat cycle.

Now, what am I going to do?

My body will only partially shift if my sexual partner is also a shifter and my soulmate. Is Misty both? If she is indeed a cat shifter, I will have to wait and see if I have triggered her heat cycle which can continue up to a week or more, until she conceives.

I have a feeling …I had better phone the clan doctor — he will know what to do.

CHAPTER ELEVEN
MISTY

WARMTH DRAPES OVER ME LIKE A SECOND SKIN, heavy and delicious, and for a long moment I float in it — boneless, humming, unwilling to move. Every inch of me feels loose and satisfied, as if my body has been thoroughly, reverently worshipped. A slow curl of pleasure stirs low in my belly, a reminder of everything that happened last night... and everything I apparently survived.

Gods, I don't even want to open my eyes. The sheets glide over my skin like warm breath, soft and decadent, and I stretch lazily into them, sighing as my muscles ripple with aftershocks. I should feel sore. I expect to feel sore in all the right places. Instead, my body feels... awakened. Hungry. Like it's already reaching for more.

And there — heat. A solid body beside me. Familiar. Male. My pulse jumps.

Braven.

His scent rolls over me, rich and wild, threaded with

something primal that makes my inner cat stretch and purr. I don't need to look to know it's him. My instincts recognise him before my mind catches up.

A wicked memory flickers — my mouth on his skin, his breath catching, running my tongue up and down his body and everywhere in between, over and over, several times more I practised to get it right. The way he tasted. The way he filled my mouth. Heat rushes through me again.

Before I can chase the thought, Braven shifts. His chest presses against my back, his arm sliding around my waist with a low, sleepy sound that vibrates against my spine. His nose brushes my neck, then his lips, then the slow drag of his tongue that sends a shiver racing down my body.

Oh. Oh, that feels unfairly good.

My breath stutters. My thighs press together. My body arches back into him without permission, seeking more of that heat, that closeness, that instinctive rightness.

Oh yes, this feels so good, but I want more, I need more. I need him inside me now...

As if he's reading my mind, Braven moves his body over mine, spreading my legs in the process. Before I can even think, he's sliding his body into mine with one hard thrust of his muscular hips, filling me to the hilt and stealing the air from my lungs.

I barely manage to suck in a much-needed breath before I scream, "Oh, Gods, yes, that feels so good. Make love to me, Braven. Oh yeah. Oh, yes. Oh, oh, oh yes, yes, Braven."

With a few well-placed thrusts, my muscles start to flutter and squeeze in a repeated sequence. I don't know what or how he did it, but Braven just made me orgasm really quickly. This man has a talent, which I could live with.

His voice slips into my mind, deep and warm, like a purr wrapped in velvet.

'Is that right, Misty?'

A tremor rolls through me. He's in my head. He's actually in my head.

'I could live with you too.'

My heart kicks hard. My eyes stay stubbornly closed.

Then his voice deepens, brushing through my thoughts with a certainty that steals the air from my lungs.

His thrusts increase becoming harder and harder. My back arching off the bed as his body moves with mine. Oh, it feels so good. Oh, Gods, his cock is hitting my cervix again. Next thing I know his cock feels like it is growing. With a long growl and hard thrust, Braven comes inside me, right into my womb. I feel a warmth increase in my belly. After finishing his own orgasm, he rolls us both, keeping our bodies together and intimately joined. With my front plastered to Braven's, I lay my head on his chest, listening to his loud racing heartbeat in my ear.

This feels so good. What a pity the doctor said I am infertile. I would not have minded having Braven's child. Oh, Gods, where did that thought come from?

'Misty... you're carrying my child. Our child. My mate. My love.'

My eyes fly open — or try to. Light floods in, too bright, and I shield my face with a groan. Bugger. Definitely not dreaming. When my vision finally adjusts, the room comes into focus: warm tones, masculine lines, a space that feels undeniably Braven.

Hang on a minute... reality begins to invade my brain. This is not... Not my Lakes Entrance apartment. It's not my hotel room.

Am I in his...His bed?

A warm hand slides over my stomach from behind, slow and reverent, and sexual tingles shoot downward in a way that makes my breath catch. My body remembers him even if my brain is still rebooting.

Images flash — his hands, his mouth, the way he moved with me like he already knew every secret my body held. The orgasms. Multiple orgasms.

Oh gods. We definitely had sex. Lots of it.

I swallow hard.

"Morning, lover," I manage, my voice embarrassingly husky. "Do we really have to wake up yet? I had the strangest dreams last night. You would not believe them. There was... a lot of sex. The best sex I have ever had, and the different sexual positions left nothing to the imagination. And how's this, you turned into a giant black cat, can you believe that?"

Braven's chest rumbles behind me — a low, amused growl that slides straight through my core.

"Misty," he murmurs, lips brushing my shoulder, "little one... that wasn't a dream."

Oh gods. The moment the words giant black cat leave my mouth, my stomach drops. Heat floods my cheeks. Did I really just say that out loud? Brilliant. Now this gorgeous, dangerous man is going to think I'm some kind of unhinged pervert with a shapeshifter kink.

I suck in a breath, trying to steady myself, trying to get ahead of the embarrassment before I have to face those eyes — those eyes that make my body forget how to behave.

"Braven, look... I'm sorry. I'm rambling. I know I'm rambling." The words tumble out of me in a rush. "It was just dreams. Really vivid, really weird dreams. I don't even remember leaving my apartment. Or getting here. Or — where is here? And what time is it? I need to get ready, I need to work, I need to—"

His hand glides over my stomach again, slow and warm, and my breath stutters. The touch is gentle, but it carries something deeper — something claiming. Something that makes my body hum in a way I don't understand.

Even though it feels so good to remain in bed, I have a lot of work to do. I wish to remain here like this for a few more minutes before facing the real world and getting up, showering and phoning the office.

Ah, hang on. Didn't I just hear Braven's voice out loud? Nah, it was in my head, I'm sure of it. Didn't he say first that he could live with me too, and what about me? Nah, that is entirely wrong, but I'm sure he said that I am pregnant? Oh boy, what did I drink last night? I must still be in la la land. "Misty," he murmurs, voice low enough to melt bone, "breathe. Let me talk."

His lips brush the side of my neck, a soft drag of heat that sends a tremor through me. My body arches before I can stop it, instinctive, needy, like he's the only thing that can quiet the ache building inside me.

"I can smell your eagerness," he whispers against my skin, and the sound of it nearly undoes me. "And yes... I want you again. But what I have to say comes first."

His body shifts behind me, unmistakably aroused, and a wave of heat rolls through me so strong I almost whimper. Where is this coming from? I've never been like this. Never wanted anyone like this. I was a virgin before arrivng in Lakes Entrance, for gods' sake. And now my body is acting like it's been waiting for him all its life.

Braven's voice deepens, threaded with something raw. "Back at the apartment... when you were open to me, your body calling to me... I couldn't hold back. And when I realised you were a virgin — Misty, I would have been gentler if I'd known."

His words hit me like a spark. My body responds before my brain can catch up, pressing back into him, seeking more of that heat, that connection, that impossible rightness. His cock slides between my arse crack. Another roll of my hips has him between my cheeks. He's like a large torpedo on a heat-seeking mission. I don't even realise I'm moving, my hips continue rolling, my body enjoying the sensations, until his breath catches.

"Misty..." His voice strains, thick with restraint. "You're making it very hard to remember we need to talk."

The air between us shifts — charged, magnetic, impossible to ignore. His hands grip my hips, steadying me, holding me still, but the tension in his body tells me exactly how close he is to losing control.

A low, rumbling growl vibrates through his chest.

Not human.

Not imagined.

Not a dream.

My heart slams against my ribs. I squeeze my eyes shut, because if I turn around and see a giant black cat in the room, I might actually pass out. And if I don't... then the truth might be even more terrifying.

Heat builds inside me, rising fast, overwhelming, a tidal wave of sensation that steals my breath. My body trembles, tightening, spiraling, and then — another orgasm hits.

Everything within me shatters.

Pleasure crashes through me in a blinding rush, stealing my voice, my breath, my thoughts. My world narrows to Braven's heat, his strength, the way he holds me like I'm something precious.

"Braven..." His name tears from my throat, raw and helpless.

He collapses against me, chest heaving, his weight warm and solid as he gathers me close. I melt into him, boneless, floating, lost in the afterglow and the impossible safety of his arms.

Sleep tugs at me again, soft and heavy.

I don't want to move. I don't want to think. I just want to stay here, wrapped in him, pretending the world outside doesn't exist.

Pretending none of this is impossible.

Pretending I didn't hear him say I'm carrying his child.

Chapter Twelve
Misty

"Hᴍᴍ... I ꜰᴇᴇʟ ꜱᴏ ɢᴏᴏᴅ."

The words slip out before I can stop them. I stretch — well, I try to — until something heavy pins my legs down. My eyes stay closed, but my senses flare. A scent rolls over me, warm and wild and unmistakably Braven. My nostrils flare on instinct.

Of course it's him.

I try stretching again, but it's useless. Something — someone — is sitting on me. And then lips brush my neck, slow and deliberate, and my whole body melts into the mattress.

"Good," Braven murmurs, sounding deliciously worn out. "You're waking up again."

Again? Oh gods.

I blink up at him, and the sight steals my breath. He's straddling my thighs, all sculpted muscle and heat, looking like he stepped straight off the cover of a magazine designed to ruin women. My gaze drags down his chest, lower, lower—

"Misty." His voice snaps me out of my ogling. I jerk my eyes back up, but it's too late. His expression shifts — serious, stern, and entirely too aware of what's going on in my head.

"Misty, stop it. Stop thinking." His tone deepens, commanding in a way that sends a shiver through me. "We have to talk. And you are not going to distract me again. Also — stop licking your lips."

I freeze mid-lick.

"For now," he adds, eyes narrowing, "that sweet tongue stays in your mouth."

A helpless hum escapes me. This man is sex on a stick, and my brain is already painting pictures of exactly what I want to do with him. Again. And again. And—

"Misty." His voice sharpens. "I said, stop thinking. Or there will be no more sex for you."

That gets my attention. My smile drops. My pout appears. He sighs. "Come on, little one. Don't be like that. We really have to talk."

Fine. Questions. I can do questions.

"Okay, Braven. How did I get here? And what time is it? The office is probably—"

He shakes his head, exasperated. What did I say now?

"Misty, just let me talk. And don't move. You're going to stay quiet and let me finish. Please."

His eyes flicker with something strained, something heavy. I want to reach up and hold him, tell him it's okay, but he told me not to move. So I nod. See? I can listen.

"Misty..." His jaw tightens. "Stop. Thinking."

I blink. Seriously?

"When you think like that," he says, voice low and rough,

"it's the same as talking out loud. You're making this impossible. You're the only person who can reduce me like this. Anyone else, I would've ripped apart by now. People take orders from me. They listen. They obey. If I say jump, they ask how high. But you—"

He cuts himself off, groaning. "Ah, you're thinking again. Please stop. I will explain everything."

I shoot him an annoyed look. I do not take orders well. He's pushing my boundaries, and he knows it.

"Misty," he warns, "you're doing it again."

I grit my teeth and try — try — to stop thinking. He'd better hurry.

He drags a hand down his face. "Misty... I can hear your thoughts. Everything you've thought since the first time we made love."

My mind screeches to a halt.

Is this guy for real or what?

"Yes," he says flatly. "I'm for real. And yes, I heard that."

Holy. Shit.

"Misty," he adds, tone stern but fighting a smile, "watch your language."

Oh, this is going to be fun. No man survives five minutes inside my head.

His eyebrow lifts. He heard that too.

Before I can spiral further, his hand slides down my thigh, fingertips brushing the scar there. Heat shoots through me so fast my toes curl.

"Misty," he warns, "stop thinking and answer my question. Do you remember when I asked about this scar?"

He pulls his hand away — damn it — and waits.

"Yes, I remember," I say, trying not to squirm. "But then you ended up... well. You know."

His look says he definitely knows.

I clear my throat. "The scar on my thigh and the one on my shoulder came from an animal attack when I was little. My parents took me to a wildlife sanctuary. I climbed through a fence and started playing with the baby cats. The panther cubs got aggressive. They attacked me. I don't remember any of it. Actually... I don't remember anything before I was eight."

Braven goes still, listening with an intensity that makes my skin prickle.

He asks quietly, "Misty... what happened to your parents?"

The question hits like a punch. Tears burn instantly. I swallow hard. Blink a few times to clear my eyes. My mind goes straight back to that time.

"I was in my last year of high school..." My voice cracks. "A month before they died, my mum took me to get a tattoo to cover the scar on my shoulder. It was one of the last things we did together."

I breathe through the ache and keep going.

"They chose the design. Said it was special. Said it represented who I am. But they never explained why."

My hands tremble. Braven covers them with his own, warm and steady.

"They left for a business trip during my exams. I stayed home to finish school. We talked on the phone the day they were coming back. They were proud of me. They told me they loved me."

The memory hits hard. I blink fast.

"A few hours later, the police came to the door. A truck driver had a heart attack. Crossed the road. Hit my parents' car."

My voice breaks. "They died instantly."

Silence settles over us, heavy and raw. Braven's grip tightens around my hands, grounding me.

"With the funeral barely over," I whisper, "I had to prove to the courts I could take care of myself. I had to draw up business plans. Sell the house. Sell the family business. I was seventeen. The judge helped me stay out of foster care." I exhale shakily. "And that's... that's how I ended up alone."

I glance back at Braven, and the look on his face nearly breaks me. Heartache sits there, raw and unguarded, and it hurts too much to stare at it head-on. I turn away, swallowing hard.

"Anyway," I whisper, forcing myself to keep going, "I was alone. Completely alone. No family. No one to fall back on." My voice wavers, but I push through it. "So I bought two apartments. Fixed them up. I live in one, rent the other. It paid itself off already."

Warm lips brush the back of my hand, soft and grounding. The touch steals my breath for a moment. I inhale slowly, steadying myself.

"And before I came here," I continue, "I signed the contracts for another apartment in the building. They're good investments. And I put myself through university. Two degrees in half the time." A shaky laugh escapes me. "Even the judge who oversaw my case was impressed. He asked me for financial advice. I doubled his retirement fund."

Braven stays silent, still straddling my legs, still watching me with that devastating expression. Tears slip down my cheeks before I even notice them. Great. Crying again.

"Misty," he says softly, "do you have any photos of your parents? I need to see them. There's something I have to check."

My head snaps toward him. "Why? Braven, why would you need to see a photo of my parents? What would that even do?"

He exhales slowly, as if choosing every word with care.

"Misty... I believe you and I used to play together." He winces. "Let me rephrase that. I believe we grew up together. As children. Right up until the day you left."

My breath catches. "What?"

His eyes lock onto mine, steady and unflinching.

"It was said that you and your parents were killed in a car accident sixteen years ago."

My stomach drops. The room tilts. "What?" My voice cracks. "Braven, I was never in a car accident. Why would you think I'm this person?"

Emotion tightens my throat. This is too much. Too fast. Too impossible.

Braven leans forward, his hands braced on either side of me, his face inches from mine. His voice is low, rough, and trembling with something I can't name.

"Because, Misty... I remember you."

Braven keeps glancing at my scar, his fingers tracing over it like he's trying to read a memory written into my skin. His brows pull together, confusion tightening his features.

"Misty," he murmurs, "I was mated — well, as mated as children can be — to my soulmate. Her name was Malisty Alexandria Ashton. Everyone called her Malisty. Or Alli." His voice softens. "She had snow-white hair. And the most beautiful blue-green eyes."

Braven lifts his gaze from my thigh and looks straight into my eyes.

"Eyes just like yours, Misty."

My breath stutters. I look away, but the name he said keeps looping in my mind. Malisty Alexandria Ashton. I don't know that name. I shouldn't know that name. But the more I repeat it, the more something inside me stirs. A tiny tug. A whisper. A blurred image of a man, a woman, a small child between them. Warmth. Safety. Love.

Braven's voice pulls me back. "Just before Malisty and her parents were killed, she and I marked each other. We mated. Too young. Far too young. I marked her here." His fingers brush my scar again, and my breath catches. "And here." His hand lifts toward my shoulder.

My heart thumps painfully. What is he saying?

"I got carried away," he admits, voice cracking. "I made the marks worse than they should've been. Our parents were furious. Malisty marked me too. You can barely see it now, but I hide it. Because it means I belong to someone. Someone I loved with everything I had. Someone who was supposed to be dead for sixteen years."

He looks up at me again, and there are tears in his eyes. Real ones. He looks lost. Completely lost.

"Braven, I—"

"No," he cuts in gently. "Let me finish."

He drags in a breath. "While you were asleep this morning, I called the doctor. He's been with my family since before my sister was born. I asked him to examine your scars. I needed to know if they matched the ones I gave Malisty. I needed to know if you're my Malisty. My soulmate."

My mind spins. Doctor? Soulmates? What is he even—

"Misty," he continues, "don't get me wrong. We are soulmates. We mated as consenting adults in your holiday apartment. We marked each other again. You bit me that night. You can feel your mark on my shoulder."

My eyes widen as he unconsciously touches the spot. Oh gods. I bit him. I actually bit him.

"Not everyone can be someone's soulmate," he says quietly. "It's rare. And for a stranger to be mine? Impossible. Unheard of. I haven't told my parents yet. The doctor swore to keep it quiet. But Misty... your scars match. Exactly. The ones on your thigh. The one on your shoulder. He kept the photos. The medical records."

My stomach drops.

"And Misty... I can only make my true soulmate pregnant. Only her. You are carrying my child."

I stare at him. My brain flatlines.

He must be joking. He has to be joking.

"Misty," he says softly, "you've been in heat for four days. You arrived in Lakes Entrance four and a half days ago. Your boss thinks you're still in meetings. After you saved his company's ass, I recommended he give you time off. And he agreed."

He pauses, glancing toward the window. Something smug flickers across his face.

"Oh, and that Kenté fellow? Fired. No one will hire him again. He came here looking for you. Found your apartment empty. He wasn't pleased. But I doubt you care."

Kenté is gone. Good riddance.

But — heat? Four and a half days? Pregnant?

Nope. Absolutely not. This guy needs a holiday.

'Misty, I told you I can hear your thoughts. And when I allow it, you can hear mine.'

I freeze. His lips didn't move.

'Yes,' Braven's voice echoes in my head, *'you can hear me. I'll teach you how to block me. It can be overwhelming.'*

Holy shit. Nope. Not happening. I'm going back to sleep. When I wake up, I'll be in my apartment, and none of this will—

"Misty," Braven says aloud, "this is real. You can hear me. You're carrying our child. And yes, I can turn into a big black cat. Anything else you want to know?"

He looks smug again. If my hands were free, I'd smack that look right off his face.

His eyebrow lifts. Challenge accepted. I raise mine right back.

Then his words replay in my head.

A big black cat.

Oh, please. As if any of this is real. If he's a big cat, then maybe that filthy guy was right about staying away from the cat.

I shoot Braven a look. "So tell me, Mister Knows-Everything... if you can turn into a big black cat, what can I do? Can I turn into one, too? Because I've never seen myself with a tail. And what about those three filthy homeless guys? Are they big cats too? Is everyone around here a big cat?"

Let's see him answer that.

My mind races, flipping through every person I've seen since arriving in Lakes. Who's human? Who's not? Who's secretly a giant cat?

Chapter Thirteen
Misty

Braven studies my face for a long moment, like he's trying to decide where to even begin. Finally, he exhales.

"Misty, I'll start at the beginning. After we were together for the first time at the apartment, you blacked out. Your body went into heat. I decided it was safer to bring you here, with your things. When you woke..." His mouth twitches. "All you wanted was more. Make love, sleep, make love, sleep. Pretty standard when a female is in heat."

Make love. Right. More like sleep — sex — sleep — sex on repeat. But sure, Braven, call it whatever helps you sleep at night.

He continues, "While you were sleeping, I called the doctor. I had to. Deep down, I knew you had to be Malisty. My Malisty. Back from the dead. My childhood soulmate. I asked him to run some tests."

Tests.

My stomach drops.

"Braven, what tests? What did he do? And please tell me you didn't just leave me alone with some stranger poking and prodding—"

"Misty." His voice softens. "I never left your side. Not for a second. But I did have to let the doctor touch you. He explained everything he needed to do before he did it. And I watched. Because you're my mate. No one touches you intimately except me."

My brain stutters. Examined. Tests. Pregnant. Soulmate.

Why? Why did I need to be examined?

And then it hits me — the thing he keeps repeating.

Pregnant.

But I'm infertile. Two specialists told me so. No ovulation. No period. No chance.

"Misty," Braven murmurs, "I can hear your thoughts. You are fertile. You just needed the right partner to stimulate your body the right way."

I choke on air.

The right partner?

"Um, Braven... are you telling me you're the magical sex partner required to activate my ovaries? Is that what I'm hearing?"

He doesn't even flinch.

"Misty, I'm a ware. A shifter. A panther. Man and cat, one mind, one body. My beast recognised you the moment we were together. My body partially shifted. And—" He hesitates, searching for words. "If you know anything about male cats, you know they have... features... that stimulate ovulation in the female."

My mind immediately conjures an image of a medieval torture device.

Fantastic.

Braven keeps going, calm as ever. "Your heat was triggered. You ovulated. We weren't using protection. And now you're pregnant."

I stare at him. No words. Just static. He must be joking. He has to be joking. This is too much. Too insane. Too—

"Misty," he says gently, "the tests show you're a cat shifter. A panther, like me. The doctor confirmed the pregnancy from your blood work. And you cannot shift right now — it could harm the baby."

My mouth opens. Nothing comes out.

"And there's more," he adds, because of course there is. "When we were children, we had a best friend. Xavier. He's a wolf shifter."

Wolves. Panthers. Soulmates. Heat.

Yep. I've officially crossed into la-la land.

"Braven," I breathe, "I need a shower. I need to brush my teeth. I need clean clothes. Food. And then I need to lie down again. And maybe — maybe — when I wake up, this will all be a weird dream."

Chapter Fourteen
Misty

My legs wobble the moment my feet sink into the soft carpet of Braven's bedroom. I'm not sure if it's the overload of information or the... activities of the last few days, but my knees feel like they're made of warm jelly.

Shock doesn't even begin to cover it.

I slip into the ensuite and close the door behind me, needing a moment — any moment — to breathe. The tap hisses to life, and the scent of the liquid soap hits me immediately. Exotic. Unexpected. Not at all what I'd imagine Braven using. I lather my hands, watching the foam swirl down the drain, trying to ground myself.

My eyes drift over his things — neat, organised, everything in its place. Toothpaste catches my attention. I swipe a bit onto my finger and scrub my teeth and tongue, desperate to feel normal for half a second. I rinse, spit, rinse again.

Normal.

Right.

As if anything about today is normal.

I step into the shower, letting the hot water pound over my head and shoulders. The heat loosens my muscles, but not my thoughts. They're a tangled mess, looping and looping.

Four days missing.

Heat.

Soulmates.

Panthers.

Pregnancy.

My mind can't keep up.

I barely register the moment Braven steps into the shower behind me. His presence fills the space instantly — warm, solid, overwhelming. His hands slide into my hair, working shampoo through it with slow, careful movements. The scent is intoxicating, something wild and earthy that makes my senses hum.

I don't know if I want him here or not. I don't know anything right now.

How did I lose days of my life?

How was I "in heat"?

How did any of this happen?

And yet... when I first saw him at the apartment, something inside me recognised him. Pulled toward him. Like coming home after being lost for years.

But the rest?

The cat-shifter stuff?

The accident?

The prophecy?

The pregnancy?

My parents never shifted. I never shifted. I don't have a tail. I don't have claws. I don't—

A thought slams into me. What if my parents weren't killed?

What if they hid us? What if they changed our names? What if they were protecting me from something?

Why didn't they tell me? Why didn't they trust me?

And then the pregnancy. How can I be pregnant? How can any of this be real?

And those filthy men at the supermarket — the ones who warned me about *"the cat."* If Braven is the cat... then what were they?

Wolves.

They must have been wolves.

My stomach drops.

Were they trying to take me to their alpha?

To mate me? To claim me?

Is that what this is? Some twisted competition? Some male dominance game?

Does Braven actually care for me — or am I just some prize?

A low, rumbling growl vibrates through the shower. I blink, dragged back to the present. The growl deepens, echoing off the tiles.

I turn slowly.

A massive black panther stands in the shower with me, water streaming down his sleek fur, ears pinned flat, eyes blazing.

My heart slams against my ribs.

"Nice kitty," I whisper.

He growls again — deeper, sharper.

Oh gods.

He shifted.

He actually shifted.

Fear spikes — then morphs into something else. Something hotter. Sharper. Angrier.

He's listening to my thoughts.

Every single one.

And he's angry about it?

My fear evaporates.

I meet his glowing eyes. "Braven... you weren't a virgin when we met, were you?"

His head dips.

My breath catches. "Don't lie to me. You've been with other women."

He lowers his head further, ears flattening.

A knife twists in my chest.

"You never waited for me," I whisper. "Not once."

He steps back, shame rolling off him in waves.

I step forward, anger burning through me like wildfire. "I didn't even know you existed, Braven. I didn't know about soulmates or shifters or any of this. And still — still — I never let anyone close. I always felt like I was waiting for someone. For you."

My voice rises over the rush of water. "And you? You just went on with your life. You slept with whoever you wanted. You didn't feel anything? Not even a hint that I was alive?"

The water shuts off with a sharp click as I hit the lever.

I step toward him, dripping, furious, betrayed.

"My mark was on you. My mark. And you still let other

women touch you. You didn't love me enough to wait. You didn't even believe in us."

His head drops lower, his whole body folding in on itself.

"Get away from me," I say, voice low and shaking. "Stop playing games with me."

He backs out of the shower, paws silent on the tiles.

And then — before my eyes — his form shimmers. Bones shift. Fur retracts. Muscles twist.

In a blink, Braven stands before me in his human skin, water dripping down his body, eyes full of something raw and broken.

Wow.

Neat trick.

Chapter Fifteen
Misty

Shock and confusion twist across Braven's face, raw and unguarded. A single tear slips down his cheek.

I stare at him.

Oh, plu- eease. Tears. Really?

But then the truth hits me like a punch to the ribs.

Oh gods. No.

No, no, no.

The look on his face — the guilt, the pleading — confirms everything I've been trying not to believe. He didn't wait for me.

My stomach twists, nausea rolling through me. My hand presses to the centre of my chest, right where the pain blooms sharp and hot. It feels like something inside me is cracking open, splintering into pieces I can't gather fast enough.

A life I never knew existed — a life we could have had — shatters before it even begins.

My anger rises like a storm.

"Give me a break, Braven," I growl, my voice low and shaking. "Tell me why I should believe a single word you say. Maybe I should go back to the car park and wait for those filthy-looking homeless guys. Or should I say wolves? Because that's what they are, isn't it?"

His eye twitches.

His hand curls into a fist, knuckles whitening.

Got you.

My body trembles, fury building with every breath. "Maybe they'll tell me the truth. Maybe their boss won't lie to me like you have. Because if there's no trust, there's no relationship. So right now? I'm leaving. I'm going home. I'm getting new tests. And if I'm pregnant — if any of this is real — I'll decide what happens next."

I snatch a towel from the rail, wrap it tight around my body, and stomp out of the bathroom. I refuse to look at him. I refuse to let him see how much this hurts.

Where are my clothes?

My bags?

My things?

"Misty, please stop." Braven steps in front of me, blocking my path. His damp hands grip my shoulders, firm and desperate. The touch sends a shiver through me — not desire, not now — but something deeper, something instinctive.

His breath comes fast. Fear shadows his face.

"You are pregnant, Misty. You can't destroy our child. Our baby is special. Our child belongs to us. I love you. I've been given a second chance to be with you."

He inhales shakily, then forces the words out.

"You're right. I did betray you with other women."

I jerk away from him, fury burning through my veins.

I waited.

I waited without knowing why.

And he—

"Misty, please," he begs. "My parents kept telling me you were dead. That my soulmate was gone. They pushed me to move on. To try. To... be with other women."

My stomach rolls. I don't want to hear this. I don't want excuses. I don't want to know what his parents wanted.

He leans closer, eyes frantic. "I never impregnated anyone else. I couldn't. Because you and I marked each other. We completed the first step of the soulmate bond. We were children — we didn't understand what we were doing. I didn't even know what sex was. I thought I'd wet myself when our parents found us."

His grip tightens. I flinch.

"I was ten, Misty. Ten. I didn't know anything. But I remember the punishment. I remember the belt. I remember not being able to sit for a week." His voice cracks. "And I remember the last time I saw you. We were crying. Clinging to each other. Our parents dragging us apart. You were screaming. I was screaming. My chest hurt so much I couldn't breathe." His eyes shine with tears.

And suddenly — images flicker through my mind.

A little boy. A little girl. Sneaking away from adults.

Giggling. Hugging. Kissing each other's cheeks. Whispering, "I love you."

Another flash — a big house. A boy's bedroom. Us hiding where we shouldn't be. Braven's excited face as he tries to show me something he shouldn't have seen. How he saw his dad doing something with a strange woman.

The memories feel real. Too real.

But...Are they mine? Or is he putting them in my head?

I don't know.

I can't tell.

Everything is too much.

The visions keep coming.

Little me. Little Braven. Sneaking into a forbidden hallway, giggling, whispering, hiding behind a half-closed door.

And then — Braven's father. Another naked woman. Her voice high and breathless, begging him not to stop. His father praising her, touching her, acting like she's the only thing in the world.

I remember being terrified. Confused. Not understanding why the woman sounded hurt.

Not understanding why Braven's father looked so... pleased. How his father enjoyed having his head between the woman's legs, and she was screaming out for Braven's father not to stop. And how I felt scared and worried about the strange moaning woman.

The scene dissolves, replaced by a little girl's bedroom. Soft colours. Toys. A tiny bed. My bed. My room. My childhood.

The little boy — Braven — grabs my hand and pulls me into another room. His face is bright with excitement, like he's discovered a secret he can't wait to share.

Then clothes are coming off — not sexual, not adult, just two children copying what they saw, trying to understand a world too big for them.

I hear my own tiny voice asking what the "dangly thing" between his legs is.

Braven giggles, explaining in the simple, innocent way only a child can.

I ask why I don't have one.

He laughs harder, telling me girls don't.

The memory shifts.

Braven gently spreads my legs, curious, examining, explaining what he thinks he knows — where wee comes from, where babies come from, where everything comes from. His touch is soft, clumsy, innocent.

Then his mouth moves to my thigh.

A sharp sting.

My small hands pushing at his head.

His grip tightening.

The pain melting into something warm and strange.

He sits up, blood on his lips, smiling proudly.

"I marked you," he says. "Forever and ever. Now you mark me."

He helps me onto his lap, guiding my legs around him, copying what he saw his father do. We hug. We kiss each other's cheeks. We giggle.

Then instinct takes over.

I lean in.

I kiss his neck.

I bite down where his shoulder meets his throat.

His blood fills my mouth.

He gasps.

I feel powerful.

Connected.

Whole.

Then pain explodes across my shoulder as he bites me back — too hard, too deep. I cry out, releasing him. We tumble to the floor. I try to crawl away, but he grabs my waist, pulling me close, instinct driving him, not understanding what he's doing.

His body presses against my back, small and frantic, trying to mimic what he saw, trying to complete something neither of us understands. He bites down on shoulder.

Then hands — adult hands — rip us apart.

Screaming.

My shoulder. Pain.

Blood.

Our parents shouting.

My heart breaking.

The memory shatters. I blink hard, dragging myself back into the present. Braven stands in front of me, eyes wide, chest heaving, waiting for my reaction.

I don't know if I want to scream or collapse.

It doens't matter, he was still with another woman.

"Braven," I whisper, voice trembling, "why did you do it? Why did you sleep with other women? Was it to punish me? For leaving you? For dying?"

He shakes his head sharply. "Misty — that was your memory. Not mine." His voice is rough, strained. "I found out later my father was having affairs. My mother isn't his soulmate. They only mated to have children. My sister and one of my brothers did the same — they fell in love with someone else and agreed to mate for children."

He steps closer, eyes locked on mine.

"But you and I... we didn't just bond. We mated.

Soulmated. Even as children, we completed the soulmate mark. That bond prevented me from impregnating another woman. My body, cat, and soul wouldn't allow it. Because my mind, my instincts, my soul — they've always belonged to you." His voice breaks. "Always, Misty."

A tear slips down Braven's cheek, carving a slow path through the water still clinging to his skin. Another follows. His face is open, raw, devastated.

"Misty," he whispers, voice cracking, "I was heartbroken. First they separated us, then your parents left with you, and then... then they told us you were dead. You and your parents. A car accident. I couldn't breathe. I couldn't think. I didn't want to live without you."

I swallow hard and look away.

Gods, does he know how impossible it is to argue with him while he's standing there naked? My eyes betray me — flicking down, then back up — and heat rushes to my cheeks.

His cheeks flush too. He disappears into the bathroom and returns with a towel slung low around his hips. Better. Worse. I don't know.

He continues, voice low and trembling. "I couldn't stay in that house. Couldn't stay near the memories. I went to a private boarding school. I tried to rebuild my life. I tried to be... normal."

His hands slide up my arms, warm and gentle, trying to anchor me. I try to pull away. He doesn't let me.

"When I turned eighteen, my parents pushed again. Told me I needed to move on. Told me I needed to... try. Older girls were thrown at me every chance they got. I resisted. For years, I resisted. But one night, I was drunk. Too drunk. And a girl—"

He swallows hard. "She climbed on me naked. I didn't want it. I didn't like it. It felt wrong. Like I was betraying you. Betraying us. I threw up, and then passed out."

My stomach twists. He wasn't bragging. He was confessing.

"Misty... it happened two more times. Different women. I woke up with them on top of me. I didn't remember choosing them. I didn't remember anything. I thought I'd just been stupid. Drunk. But I regretted it. Every time."

A cold shiver runs through me.

His words make me pause. How can he not remember? Something does not sit right. It sounds more like he was drugged. Someone set him up.

The question would be — was it his parents? Would they do something so low, and have their son drugged?

He hears the thought. His jaw tightens.

"You're right," he murmurs. "There's more." My breath catches. "For the last ten months, I was seeing someone. Liasa." I knew it. "She's a leopard shifter. We met while I was away. We thought we were falling in love, but... it wasn't real. Something was missing in our relationship. She saw your mark on me. She knew I had a soulmate. She wanted to try for a baby anyway. To see if I was capable."

He looks down, shame flickering across his face.

"We tried for months. Nothing happened. She grew depressed. Angry. Two weeks before you arrived, I found her in my bed with someone else."

My jaw drops. Seriously. A woman who was meant to be in love with him and she has sex with another man, in Braven's bed.

What kind of woman does that?

"Liasa wanted children. If I couldn't give her that, she didn't want me. That was her line in the sand."

How selfish. Cruel. Heartless. Is this woman?

I open my mouth to ask where she is now — but I don't need to. He hears the thought. "We bit each other," he admits quietly. "We mated. But I never felt the bond. Not like ours. Not even close. I haven't heard from her since I kicked her out and all her belongings. And I don't want to."

My eyes flick around the room — the furniture, the bed, the bathroom. She was here. In this house. In his life.

Before I can speak, he rushes on. "When I saw her with someone else, I had everything removed. Everything she touched. The house was stripped of everything, and it was thoroughly cleaned. New furniture. New appliances. New tiles. New lined. New everything. I couldn't stand the scent of her. I needed her presence gone."

My gaze drifts to the towel around his hips, the bathroom behind him, the bed we've shared.

All new.

All untouched by her.

My stomach still twists, but the nausea softens.

"Misty," he whispers, stepping closer, "I want to be with you. You're my soulmate. My one and only. You make me whole. You make me feel alive again. I don't want anyone else. Ever." His voice breaks. "And you're carrying our baby. Our miracle. Something I've wanted my entire life. Something I thought I'd never have. I love you, Misty. I've missed you for sixteen years. And now you're here. You're right here."

Before I can react, he moves — fast, instinctive — wrapping his arms around me. His warmth surrounds me, his face buried in my damp hair, his breath brushing my ear. A shiver races down my spine. His scent fills my lungs, rich and intoxicating, and my emotions spiral.

Anger.

Fear.

Longing.

Love.

Confusion.

All tangled together.

Oh gods.

What am I going to do?

CHAPTER SIXTEEN
MISTY

I EASE MYSELF OUT OF BRAVEN'S ARMS, INCH BY INCH, until the warmth of him slips away. The loss hits harder than I expect — a sudden coldness, a hollow ache — but I push it down. I'm too overwhelmed, too wrung out, too full of questions and fear and anger to let myself melt into him again.

I need space.

I need air.

I need to think.

My parents always said you don't find answers at the bottom of a bottle, and right now I cling to that memory like a lifeline. No scotch. No drowning. Just... movement. Action. Something to ground me.

Clothes.

I need clothes.

Braven must hear the thought because he steps back immediately and gestures toward a corner of the room. My bags. My things. All neatly stacked.

Smart man.

Never mess with a pissed-off female.

I grab clean clothes and retreat to the bathroom. The moment the door clicks shut, I breathe easier. I dress quickly, pulling on jeans and a soft top, then find my makeup case tucked into the vanity. The familiar routine steadies me — hair into a ponytail, teeth brushed with my own toothbrush, my own toothpaste, my own minty freshness. Moisturiser. Foundation. A sweep of eyeshadow. A line of eyeliner. Mascara. Lipstick. Deodorant.

By the time I'm done, I look like me again.

Or at least a version of me that isn't falling apart.

Back in the bedroom, I spot my briefcase. Relief washes through me. I open it, scanning the contents. Everything seems intact — except my phone. Panic spikes until I find my handbag buried under my clothes. My phone is inside, I turn it on and check — battery half full.

Good.

One thing in my life isn't a disaster.

I walk through the house — gods, it's huge — until I find the dining room. The table is long, oval, polished teak. New. Everything here is new. No trace of Liasa. No trace of anyone but Braven.

I set my briefcase down, pull out my paperwork, and start sorting. Contracts. Portfolios. Notes. My hands move automatically, muscle memory taking over while my brain tries to catch up with the last four days of my life.

The original contracts are missing.

Of course they are.

Another thing to ask Braven.

My stomach growls loudly enough to echo off the walls. I glance at my phone. An hour and a half has passed. And the date—

My breath catches.

Four days.

Four days gone.

I push back from the table, dizzy. I need food. Water. Something to keep me upright. I stand, ready to hunt down the kitchen, when—

"Ahh!" I yelp, nearly toppling off the chair.

Braven's voice vibrates through the room, deep and warm and far too close.

"I heard that, Misty. I'm already on my way with food."

I whip my head toward the doorway. Braven stands there holding a tray — sandwiches, juice, glasses. His smile is soft, hopeful, careful.

"Misty, I hope you like roast beef sandwiches and orange juice. Your thoughts were loud, but your stomach was louder."

Despite everything, a tiny smile tugs at my lips.

He's trying.

He really is.

But I still need space.

"Braven... thank you. Really. But I need time. I need to breathe. I need to understand what's happening to me. I just found out I'm half panther. That I'm not fully human. That we're soulmates. That I'm pregnant. That I've lost four days of my life. And every time you're near me, I either want to curl up in your lap or drag you into the nearest bed."

His eyes darken at that, but I push on.

"I need to sort out my work. I need to talk to your doctor.

And I need to see my own doctor too. No offence, but I don't know your family doctor. I'll feel better getting a second opinion."

His face falls.

The sadness in his eyes is like a physical blow. I look away before I crumble.

"Misty," he says quietly, "when I brought you here, I looked through your briefcase. I reviewed everything you prepared. I was impressed. Truly. I showed my family. Within an hour, the new contracts were signed and sent back to your company."

My jaw drops. He's been through my briefcase...

He continues, "I also called your CEO. I arranged a conference call. I told them about your work. About your professionalism. About Kenté's sabotage. I requested you stay on for a couple more weeks to help with new ventures."

My mouth hangs open. I snap it shut. "Ah... thank you, Braven."

He steps closer, slow and careful, like approaching a frightened animal. He leans down and presses a soft kiss to my forehead. His arms wrap around me, warm and strong, and my body betrays me — relaxing into him, breathing him in, wanting him.

His scent curls through me, rich and intoxicating. My hormones surge. My legs want to wrap around him. My hands want to pull him closer. My heart wants to trust him.

But my stomach growls again, loud and insistent.

Braven chuckles softly against my hair. "Come on, Misty," he murmurs. "Eat."

And gods help me... I think I want to. Because I am hungry.

Chapter Seventeen
Misty

Once the sandwiches and juice settle in my stomach, I dive straight back into my list.

Work mode. Safe mode.

The only mode that doesn't make me want to scream or cry or throw myself into Braven's arms like some hormonal lunatic.

Emails.

Phone calls.

Damage control.

I sit at Braven's dining table, laptop open, papers spread everywhere like I'm trying to run a corporate office out of a country cabin. The house is quiet except for the soft hum of the fridge and the occasional creak of old timber settling. It should be calming. It isn't.

LJ's frantic messages flash across my screen like a siren. Four days gone and she's spiralled into full disaster mode. If I don't call her now, she'll have the police, the army, and possibly a psychic on standby.

I hit call.

She answers before the first ring finishes. "LITTLE KITTY GIRL—where have you been? Four days, Misty! I was about to plaster your face on missing posters!"

I wince. "LJ, breathe. I'm okay."

"You are not okay. People who are okay don't vanish for nearly a week. I thought you'd been abducted by a cult, or murdered, or—"

"LJ." I pinch the bridge of my nose. "I'm fine. I promise. I just... had a lot going on."

Yeah, nah.

Not mentioning anything about almost getting cornered by three homeless-looking maybe-shifters outside the supermarket.

That's a fast track to LJ staging an intervention and dragging me to a witch doctor for a brain cleanse.

She huffs, unconvinced. "What aren't you telling me?"

"Nothing," I lie, pacing because my nerves won't let me stay still. "I just need time to sort things out."

She goes quiet for a beat. "You sound weird."

I hesitate. Then sigh. "I met someone."

A gasp. Then a shriek so loud I yank the phone away from my ear. Seriously...what are you, three, LJ?

"WHAT? You disappear for four days and ctell me you met a man? Is he hot? He better be hot—"

"He's... yeah." Heat crawls up my neck. "He's very hot."

Visions of Braven naked with water droplets sliding down his....

She squeals again. "Little Kitty Girl, I don't know whether to ground you or celebrate you."

"It's complicated," I mutter. Shaking my head from the naked visions.

"Oh, I'm getting every detail," she says. "Next week. In person. With snacks. And a whiteboard. Oh, and wine. Lots of wine and cheese."

"Fine," I say, smiling despite everything. "Next week."

"And Misty?"

"Yeah?"

"Don't vanish on me again. I nearly hexed half the town."

A laugh escapes me. "I won't. Promise."

We hang up, and the moment the call ends, the real world slams back into place. My phone battery is clinging to life, so I plug it in and watch the little charging symbol blink on.

One tiny thing cooperating.

I sit back down at Braven's table, crack my knuckles, and open the next email.

My phone buzzes again.

> LJ:
>
> If you disappear again, I'm changing your Netflix password.
>
> Don't test me, Little Kitty Girl.

Several seconds later, another buzz.

> LJ:
>
> Also, if this mystery man is the reason you went off-grid, I'm putting you on one of those toddler leashes.
>
> Pick a color.

A snort bursts out of me before I can stop it. Great. Now

I'm laughing alone in a panther-shifter's dining room like a lunatic.

I shake my head, swipe the notifications away, and dive back into the inbox.

Work mode. Safe mode. The only mode I can control. repeats in my head.

Now...Focus. Back to emails.

One from The Judge catches my eye, sitting there like it's judging me through the screen.

Of course he's heard about Kenté. Of course he's disappointed I didn't come to him.

I roll my eyes and sink deeper into the chair. I'm not about to drag him into office politics. He's retired. He deserves peace. And I've always handled my own battles, even when they leave bruises no one sees.

I open the email anyway and scan his words.

His tone is exactly what I expect—stern, paternal, and laced with that quiet authority that once made grown lawyers sweat through their suits. He wants to help. He's frustrated I didn't ask. He's worried.

I type out a polite thank-you, add a couple of stock tips he'll appreciate, and casually slip in a line about having met someone new.

A man. A very distracting one.

Hopefully that's enough to stop him from trying to set me up with every eligible bachelor in Melbourne. The man means well, but he treats my love life like a community service project.

I hit send.

Now, back to my overflowing inbox, the dining table still covered in paperwork, and the world still spinning faster than I can keep up with. But at least one email is handled. One tiny corner of the chaos is under control.

My stress motto — Work mode. Safe mode — The only mode I can cling to when stress comes knocking.

NOW BACK TO BUSINESS.

I scroll through the documents spread across Braven's dining table, the screen glow reflecting off the polished wood. Everything is lined up, organised, efficient. My life might be a tornado right now, but my real estate portfolio is thriving.

Thank the gods for technology.

A few calls, a video meeting, a digital signature, and the contractors are off and running. Two months and the place will be gutted and rebuilt exactly how I want it. Paint, carpet, tiles, appliances — every detail already chosen, already matched to the other apartments. Easy. Familiar. Mine.

Apartment three — purchased. Tick

Settlement — complete. Tick

Keys — ready for pickup. Tick

Builder — already contracted. Thank god. Tick

Renovation plans — finalised. Finally, yes! Tick

Safe room — approved. Double big tick.

By the time I finish the last conference call, my brain feels like it's been wrung out and hung up to dry. I close the laptop and let my eyes fall shut for a moment.

Now it's time to focus on me.

On my health.

On the question that's been sitting in the centre of my chest like a ticking bomb. Am I pregnant or not?

I don't feel different. No nausea. No dizziness. No cravings. No nothing.

Except... When Braven holds me, something shifts inside me. Something warm. Something protective. Something that feels like it's not just me anymore.

But that could just be hormones.

Or shock.

Or the mate-bond.

Or the fact that my entire life has been flipped upside down and shaken like a snow globe.

There's only one way to know for sure.

I stand, take a slow breath, and press a hand to my stomach.

Time to find out the truth

I STARE AT THE PIECE OF PAPER ON THE DINING TABLE like it's about to bite me.

Braven's handwriting.

His family doctor's name.

A phone number that suddenly feels heavier than my briefcase.

What am I going to do?

My fingers drum against the wood, restless, jittery. I could drive back to Melbourne. I could see my own specialist. Someone I trust. Someone who knows my history. Someone who doesn't belong to this... world.

But then again — what good is a human doctor if I'm not fully human?

Bugger it.

I grab the paper and my phone before I can talk myself out of it. My thumb hovers over the keypad, my pulse thudding in my ears. I need answers. I need to know what's happening to my body. I need to know if I'm pregnant. I need to know if everything Braven said is real or if I'm losing my mind.

I start dialing. One number. Then the next. Then the next.

My breath catches in my throat. This is it. No turning back now. I lift the phone to my ear, bracing myself for whatever comes next.

Chapter Eighteen
Braven

What am I going to do?

The question loops through my mind like a rotating blade. I've screwed up. Badly. And now my mate — my soulmate — is here, alive, breathing, carrying our cub, and I'm standing in the ruins of every mistake I've ever made.

How is she ever going to forgive me?

The truth is ugly. I always knew, deep down, that Malisty wasn't gone. My beast never accepted her death. Not once. But with my parents pushing, the clan whispering, everyone telling me to move on, to "live again," I let myself be dragged into a life that wasn't mine.

And Misty — my Misty — stayed faithful without even knowing who she was waiting for.

I shake my head, disgust curling in my gut. I was engaged. Engaged. To someone who wasn't my mate. Someone who never held even a fraction of my heart.

Misty's voice drifts down the hallway, animated and bright

as she handles her phone calls. I pause, listening. Pride swells in my chest. My little mate is sharp, organised, brilliant. She's not with me for money — she has her own. And she saved my family's finances without even realising it.

If it weren't for her, we'd still be bleeding money.

By the time I finish going through the folders — folders I removed from my mate's briefcase, my pulse is pounding in my ears.

My father.

My own father. He has more than one secret portfolio. Hidden money. A lot of secret money, and it started with the pack's money. Quiet transactions here and there. A trail he clearly never expected anyone to follow.

And Marcus.

My idiot little brother — who apparently isn't an idiot at all. He has played me like a fool, crying poor.

His portfolio is over two years old. Two years of steady growth. Two years of bonuses. Two years of pretending to be broke while he's sitting on a small fortune.

No wonder Liasa was sniffing around him. She knew exactly what she was doing.

I sit back, rubbing a hand over my face. My family is a mess. A secretive, manipulative, money-hoarding mess. And Misty — my Misty — walked straight into the middle of it and somehow managed to untangle everything in a matter of hours.

I'm grateful she brought these folders.

Grateful she's brilliant. Grateful she's mine. My mate.

But the relief doesn't last long. Because the truth hits me again — hard. I can't let her leave.

If she walks out that door, I'll lose her. Forever. And what happens to our cub? What happens to the tiny life growing inside her? What happens to the future I've dreamed of since I was ten years old?

I press my palms to my eyes, trying to breathe.

I need to talk to the doctor. I need to know if there's a way to unlock her memories. To free her cat. To help her shift. To make her whole again.

Whatever happened to her after she left here — it blocked her. Caged her and her cat. And that isn't healthy for her or our cub. I have to fix it. I have to protect her.

And I have to remember to call her Misty — not Malisty. Her new name. Her new life. The life she built without me.

I don't know how to tell my family about her. I can't tell them Malisty's alive. I can't tell them my soulmate has returned from the dead.

They'll ask questions I can't answer. Questions I won't answer.

And then there's the biggest problem of all.

X.

My stomach drops.

If the wolves are sniffing around, X won't be far behind. He'll feel the pull. He'll recognise it instantly. He'll know exactly who she is — our mate. And if he remembers the bite on his little finger...

Shit.

Shit.

Shit.

He'll come for her.

He'll come for us.

I can't let that happen.

That's it. I will be going back to Melbourne with Misty. Not just her, but, us. Back to her world. Back the city — Melbourne together. Away from the clans. Away from danger. Away from X.

I hear Misty's voice again — soft, polite, professional — making an appointment with the pack doctor. Good. She needs answers. She needs someone who understands shifter biology.

But she also needs me. I push off the wall, ready to go to her, when my phone rings from the other room.

The ringtone freezes me.

Mother.

Oh, perfect.

I grit my teeth, inhale slowly, and force my voice into something calm.

I need to play nice.

Just long enough to get Misty out of here.

I answer the call.

"Mother."

CHAPTER NINETEEN
MISTY

I WAIT IN THE CROWDED DOCTOR'S CLINIC, surrounded by other women and their annoying young children. My patience is wearing thin. How can people handle these whinging little brats? I lift my handbag off the floor and place it firmly back on my lap. Why do I have the feeling that if I leave anything on the floor, one of these little germ-infested criminals will have it emptied and spread across the tiles within minutes?

A snotty little boy waddles closer, his eyes weeping, nose leaking, mouth open in a sticky half-cry. My stomach rolls. I cringe inside and shift my feet away from him like he's radioactive. Geez, what germs is this kid sharing... gross.

By three-thirty, I've found the latest issue of Dolly magazine in the paper rack — *"latest"* meaning at least five years old — but it's better than staring at the plague carriers roaming and a few of the Oprah-screaming delinquents in the room. I sink back into one of the beige chairs, flipping through outdated hairstyles and quizzes, trying to distract myself from the doctor's earlier comment about wanting to see me without Braven.

Movement catches my eye. Someone clears their throat. I glance up from the article I'm pretending to read and see a nurse standing in the doorway. Her gaze sweeps the room, passes over me, then snaps back like she's spotted prey.

"Misty Statesly, please. Come this way."

I nod, smile politely, and say, "That's me."

It takes effort — real effort — to weave around the sticky-fingered rug rats reaching for my legs like I'm a climbing frame. I follow the nurse through the doorway, relieved to escape the germ fog.

Inside the exam room, the nurse shuts the door and gestures to the scale. "Shoes, jacket, anything heavy, place over there. Pointing to a chair."

Great. If I'd known I was being weighed, I would've skipped lunch. Or breakfast. Any food for the last week.

I strip off what I can and step onto the scale.

I blink and refocus on the numbers.

What the...? Down five kilos. Since when?

I blink again at the number, in case I'm reading it wrong. That can't be right. I don't lose weight like this. Not without trying.

Nurse Shannon — as she introduced herself — notices my expression. "Everything alright?"

"Oh... um. I usually weigh more than this. I've lost five kilos since last week."

She smiles, jotting it down like it's nothing. I slip my clothes and shoes back on, and she hands me a specimen jar.

"Bathroom's just there."

Fantastic. Pee in a cup. My favourite past time.

It doesn't take long. I wash my hands, open the door, and hand her the jar. She turns to her workstation, dipping strips into the sample. My gaze drifts — and freezes.

A pregnancy test sits on the bench.

I watch as she also adds a few drops from my specimen jar to the pregnancy test.

My pregnancy test.

It's not long before the little screen flashes a symbol.

Positive.

My breath stops. My chest tightens. My vision tunnels.

Oh, shit.

Oh... shit.

This can't be mine. It has to belong to someone else. But the room is empty. Just me. Just Shannon, the nurse. And the beacon, *"What the hell is happening here?"* — my pregnancy test.

I'm pregnant!

Braven was right. I'm actually pregnant.

Oh my fucking gods.

My breathing spikes. My heart races. My hands shake. Panic claws up my throat.

I take a step back, hand pressed to my chest. Am I having a heart attack? A panic attack? Both?

Focus, Misty. Breathe. You need answers.

Nurse Shannon scribbles notes, then turns with a bright smile. "Congratulations! Your test is positive. The doctor will see you shortly. And since you're pregnant, you'll need to drink both of these bottles of water. He'll want to run another test."

My hands move automatically, taking the bottles even though I feel like I might drop them.

Nurse Shannon picks up the test and my file, opens the door, and walks out — leaving me alone with my spiralling thoughts and a bladder that's already protesting.

Chapter Twenty
Braven

WITH MIXED EMOTIONS TWISTING THROUGH ME, I drop Misty off at the doctor's clinic. I prefer to stay with her, only for Misty to push the issue as she climbs out of the car, informing me she is a grown woman and has been looking after herself for a long time. She can handle the doctor's clinic all by herself, and she does not require any assistance from me as she is not a child.

Does she even realise how hard it is to leave her anywhere by herself? My other half, my cat, is going stir crazy. He wants out so he can protect his mate — our mate.

If it is not for Mum phoning, I would follow Misty into the clinic. So here I am, pulling up at my parent's exuberant three-story family home, situated on an eight-hundred-acre bush property.

Pity. While I am growing up here, surrounded by this large house and bushland, throughout the years, it never feels like a family home. There is no love, only a power play — cruelty. If you show weakness, you are punished.

When I was devastated after the death of Malisty, my father wanted to beat me until I no longer cried. He tried to make a man out of me. A ten-year-old boy, losing a part of his soul, and all my father wanted to do was beat me to make me stronger, not believing in the connection between two soulmates.

We were told Malisty and her parents died in a car accident. I remember the way the elders delivered the news — flat, final. I remember the way my chest caved in, the way my cat howled inside me, the way I could not breathe. I was devastated with the news. As if that even touched the truth. My father saw my grief as weakness. Another excuse to punish.

Now I know Misty is alive. Breathing. Stubborn. Sitting in a doctor's clinic telling me she does not need me. The lie about the car accident sits like a stone in my gut.

She has no memory of her early childhood. No memory of shifters. No memory of me. No memory of being Malisty — my mate. And no one else knows she is alive.

Climbing the front steps, I survey my surroundings, noticing another security camera has been installed since I was here last. Just as I take another step forward, Marcus appears in the doorway, standing in his six-foot-two height. My father always picked on Marcus, and when I was able to, silly me would protect my baby brother.

In the end, when I was home, it was I receiving the beatings and punishments my so-called alpha and father had in store for Marcus. By the time Marcus turned sixteen, I had made the hard decision to stop stepping in and taking the punishments meant for someone else. I had more pressing matters to deal with.

My father wanted me to learn how to be the next alpha, which meant Marcus had to learn to change his life and prevent my father from coming after him.

Whatever beliefs my father has had, his sick and perverted treatment of his children will end with his death. When I take over and become alpha, no person in this clan will treat one of their children the same way my father treated my siblings and me.

"Braven, good to see you here, Bro. Father wants to discuss a few clan matters with you. He also wants to know what you are going to do about Liasa."

With my head shaking in annoyance and my eyes narrowing at my younger brother, I keep walking and step into the house without speaking to Marcus.

"Braven, are you going to say hello to me or are you still keeping your distance?"

I turn and give my head a slight shake toward Marcus' direction to indicate that I am not speaking with him.

"Okay. I'll take that as you are not speaking with me yet. But how many times do I have to say how sorry I am. If I could take those... I mean that day back, I would."

Hmm. Sorry. Whatever you reckon, little Bro. That was not the first time Marcus had slept with Liasa. But then, I had already worked that out for myself. They had been far too comfortable with one another in my bed when I had seen them.

My instincts are warning me to keep clear and not to trust Marcus with a ten-foot pole. My little Bro has manipulated me enough over the years. I have the feeling he used to get a kick out of seeing me taking his punishments for him.

I think it is time to send off a quick text to my head of security, to inform them that my brother Marcus is not allowed to enter my home, and to change my locks again. Something is definitely not right where Marcus is involved. And to find Liasa, I think it is time to know what that bitch is up to. A thorough background search on both of them is required, something I should have performed weeks ago.

My thumb hesitates for a moment as another thought hits — if they believed Malisty died, if they told me she died, then someone out there knows more than they should. Someone knows she survived. Someone knows she is Misty, but who?

I place my phone on silent after notifying Misty I am at my parents' house. And for her to text me when she is finished, only for Misty to reply with:

MISTY:

Still at the doctor's clinic. Don't worry about me. I'll pick up my car from the holiday apartment complex once I'm finished with the appointment. I'll meet you back at your house.

My blood pressure rises. Misty knows how to push my buttons. To make matters worse, I do not want her driving around alone with the wolves sniffing about, especially when they have already tried to take her once.

My grip tightens around the phone until the casing creaks. My cat rakes claws down my insides, demanding I turn around, demanding I forget this house, this family, this so-called alpha training, and go back to our mate.

The scent of polish and old wood hits me as I move deeper into the foyer. Voices drift from my father's office — low, controlled, the kind that always precede orders and punishments. My shoulders tense automatically, muscle memory from a childhood spent bracing for impact.

I pause just inside the doorway, Misty's text burning in my mind, the memory of being told she died when I was ten, overlaying the image of her sitting in a sterile waiting room, alive and stubborn and mine.

This is one secret I will be keeping from my family. No one here knows she is alive. No one knows she is my soulmate, Malisty.

My cat settles into a cold, lethal focus.

One thing at a time. I deal with the alpha. See what he wants. And then I make damn sure no one ever comes near Misty again.

CHAPTER TWENTY-ONE
BRAVEN

"BRAVEN, WHAT HAS YOU SO FOCUSED?" MY mother's voice slices through the hallway like a blade. Sharp. Cold. Too close.

I jump before I can stop myself. Damn it. I need to be more alert in this house. I turn slowly, schooling my expression. She stands there with her arms folded, eyes narrowed, already judging, already prying.

"Marcus informed me you haven't seen Liasa for weeks. Why is that? Your father said you cancelled the mating. Why?"

Of course. No hello. No, how are you? Just straight into the interrogation.

"Mother," I say, keeping my tone flat, "I told you. I broke up with Liasa. I don't love her. I cancelled the mating. She wanted children, and I can't give her any."

Her eyes sharpen. "Have you even tried?"

What. Is she serious?

Before she can launch into one of her rants, I cut her off.

"Mother, you know I can only impregnate my soulmate. Liasa is not my soulmate."

Her mouth opens, but I don't let her speak.

"And before you defend her — she was sleeping around. I saw it. With my own eyes. So if she's pregnant, it's not mine."

Shock flickers across her face. She wasn't expecting that. Good. I pull out my phone, swipe to the photo, and hold it up in front of her. Her eyes widen. Her breath catches. Her face drains of colour.

Yes, Mother. Look closely. That's your precious youngest son screwing my fiancée in my bed.

"As you can see," I say calmly, "that photo was taken in my house. In my bedroom. And you wonder why I don't trust Liasa."

She stares at the screen, horrified.

"And the other person?" I continue. "He knows I know. I told him to expect a call from Liasa. She's probably pregnant with Marcus by now."

"But... how—"

"No." My voice snaps like a whip. "Do not cover for Marcus. He made his choices. Now he can deal with the consequences."

I shake my head, disgust curling in my gut. "Liasa and I tried for months. Nothing. Her period arrived right after the last time we were together — so I know she wasn't pregnant. And I've seen the new bite mark on her thigh. That one isn't mine."

Mother's face twists — shock, anger, humiliation, all fighting for dominance. For a moment, she looks almost... human.

Almost.

I slide my phone back into my pocket. "Oh, and Mother," I add, turning away, "I have multiple copies of those photos. You don't think that's the only one, do you?"

Her breath hitches. I don't wait for a response. I turn my back on her and walk toward my father's office, each step steady, controlled, deliberate. Let her choke on the truth.

I have bigger things to deal with. Misty. Our cub. The wolves. X.

And gods help anyone who tries to take what's mine.

I stop in front of my father's office door and consider turning around. Walking away. Pretending I never came.

But I'm not a coward. And avoiding him only delays the inevitable. My skin crawls before I even knock. I can hear him inside — not working, not leading, not doing anything remotely alpha-like. Unless you're my father, fucking anything in a short skirt. Doesn't matter if they are willing or not.

Of course, he would be fucking another woman in my mother's house.

In my mother's house. He doesn't care. She's turned a blind cheek for years.

I rap my knuckles against the hardwood.

"Come in, Braven."

I open the door — and there she is. Gurgette. One of the clan women who's been warming my father's bed for years. And by the smell of it, she's just finished giving him a blowjob.

My father smirks. "Come in, Braven. Close the door. I think you already know Gurgette."

I nod once. "Yes. I've noticed Gurgette around the grounds."

I turn my head just enough to look at her — at the streak of my father's cum sliding down her chin.

Disgust twists in my gut.

"Gurgette," I say, voice cold, "I think it's time for you to leave and clean yourself up. And wipe your face while you're at it. My father's cum running down your chin isn't a good look. Especially when my mother is just down the hall. This is her house."

Her eyes widen. Her hand flies to her face. She looks embarrassed — good. She should be.

I open the door wider, giving her the hint.

She glances at my father, but he doesn't lift a finger to help her. Of course, he doesn't. She scrambles to her feet, yanks her dress down, and rushes past me. I slam the door shut behind her.

My father watches me with that smug, oily expression he's perfected over the years. I wait. I learned long ago that speaking first is a mistake.

"So, my son," he drawls. "You have impeccable timing. If you'd been ten minutes later, I could've fucked her up the arse."

I shake my head, disgust crawling up my spine.

"Really, Father?" I deadpan. "Do you even know where she's been? Who she's been fucking?"

His face doesn't change. He doesn't care. He never has.

"So enough about the little slut," he says. "I understand you're no longer mated with Liasa. Why is that?"

Is it broken-record day? I pull out my phone, swipe to the photos, and forward them to him.

A ding sounds from somewhere under the piles of rubbish

on his desk. He digs through the mess, finds his phone, taps the screen.

His eyebrows rise. Then rise higher.

Then he looks at me. "Okay," he says finally. "I get it. Your fiancée is a cheating bitch."

"Ex-fiancée," I correct.

"I take it this is your house. Your bed."

"Yes. They were too busy to notice me walk in."

"What did you say to them?"

"Nothing." I shrug. "I took photos, removed my engagement ring, and left. When I came back, they were gone. I packed her things, replaced everything in the house, and had it cleaned top to bottom. I didn't want a trace of either of them left."

He nods. "The elders informed me the mating was cancelled. This is one area where the alpha has no say. I would have told you to remain with her."

I stare at him, incredulous. "You have to be joking. I'm not staying with a woman who cheats. She's probably pregnant with Marcus. I'm not claiming someone else's cub."

"Really? Then what are you going to do? If you want to take over as alpha, you need a mate. And you need to prove you can father a cub."

He thinks he knows everything. He knows nothing.

"Look, Father." I rake a hand through my hair. "I met someone. It's early days, but I think she might be my soulmate."

He bursts out laughing. The urge to smash my fist into his face is almost overwhelming.

"You?" he sneers. "You think you've found your soulmate? You had one, boy. And she's dead."

My jaw tightens. My pulse spikes. My cat snarls inside me.

"Dad," I say quietly, "I'm positive this woman is my second chance. She's at the doctor's right now, confirming what I already know."

His eyes narrow. "Confirming what?"

Shit. I've said too much. Too soon, too fast.

"I mated with her. She went into heat. I'm positive she's pregnant with my cub."

The smugness drains from his face. "Who is she?" he demands.

Warning bells scream in my head. I keep my voice steady. "Believe it or not, our financial planner is a shifter. She didn't know. She's never shifted. But when we joined, I partially shifted and triggered her heat. That only happens with another shifter, especially your mate. She's my mate. My soulmate."

His mouth falls open. "You partially shifted? You're telling me your dick partially shifted?"

"Yes, Father," I say flatly. "My dick partially shifted."

He grunts. "I wondered why you stopped coming into the office. Thought you were with Liasa again."

I shake my head. "Never again."

He leans back, eyes calculating. "Alright, son. I want to meet your new soulmate. And we still need to go over the other portfolios she mentioned. Might as well increase the clan's wealth before she leaves her company."

His tone is too sweet. Too eager. Too dangerous. Every instinct I have screams that he's planning something. I nod anyway. For now, I play along.

But Misty will never be alone with him. Not for a second.

CHAPTER TWENTY-TWO

MISTY

WITH MY FOOT TAPPING AGAINST THE FLOOR, I SIT IN the doctor's consulting room, waiting for the person who's about to confirm the truth I'm still struggling to accept. One bottle of water is empty. The second is half gone. My bladder is screaming.

The door clicks. A stranger walks in. I jump so violently I nearly fall off the chair. He walks behind his desk. He's tall — over six foot — with a buzz-cut, square jaw, broad shoulders, and piercing green eyes that seem to look straight through me. The stranger sits down. I search his face, trying to place him, trying to sense what kind of shifter he is.

He smiles. "Good afternoon, Misty. It's good to see you all grown up and conscious. I'm pleased you arrived without Braven."

So he knows me. From childhood.

"Afternoon, Doctor. I'm here for answers. You said you

knew me as a child. I don't remember anything before I was eight years old. I left here at... six? What can you tell me?"

He studies me. "I will only use your current name. No one will hear your true identity from me. When I heard about the accident that supposedly killed you and your parents, I was shocked. As Braven's treating doctor, I knew you couldn't be dead. If you had died, the bond would have killed him too."

A gasp escapes me. Braven... could have died.

He continues, "I still had a sample of your blood. I tested it under a different name. I needed to know why your parents staged your deaths. I concluded it had to be because of you — something dire."

"What kind of tests?" My voice is barely a whisper.

"The usual. And a few unusual." His expression darkens. "After some time, I found my answer. I know why your parents hid you. And no, I haven't told Braven."

"Why not? What did the tests reveal?"

"When the time is right, I'll tell you. Not here. Not today. There is trouble brewing. If the information I know is revealed, you would likely have a kill order placed on your head."

I freeze. A kill order. On me.

"Is it contagious? Deadly?"

"No. Not contagious. Not deadly per se. But your life is in danger. When are you returning to Melbourne?"

"Tonight or tomorrow. Why? If no one knows my results—"

"Misty, because of your results, the wolves will be sniffing around—"

"You're too late. They already tried to grab me the day I arrived. I fought two of them. The third just watched." He doesn't look surprised. "Why am I so special to the wolves?" I demand.

He doesn't answer my question. Instead, says, "Braven told me you reinforced your mating bites. And that you've never shifted."

I shake my head.

"You didn't know about shifters before coming here this week?"

Another shake.

"Your parents hid our world from you. Someone blocked your animal. Do you know any witches?"

My breath catches. "Witches? You're kidding me." Since when are witches real?

His expression tells me I said too much out loud.

Oops.

FORTY MINUTES LATER, I WALK OUT OF THE CLINIC with an empty bladder, a spinning head, and more questions than answers.

The doctor confirmed the pregnancy again. Gave me the test. Performed an ultrasound *"to check my uterus."*

Printed a tiny grainy blob picture.

My blob.

He asked if I'd had unprotected sex in the last twelve hours.

I admitted Braven and I had been... busy. He warned I could still conceive another cub within twenty-four hours.

Fantastic. Multiples. Just what I need.

He promised to email my blood results — anonymously — because if anyone finds out... Danger will be my new name.

I buy the pregnancy vitamins he recommends and I start walking toward the accommodation apartments. I need air. I need space. I need time to think — and there are things the doctor told me that I need to keep from Braven until I understand them myself.

By the time I reach the undercover car park, my head is pounding.

My phone vibrates. I swipe the screen. Braven's message fills my vision.

> **BRAVEN:**
>
> Misty, do not go back to my house. Pick up your car. I cannot speak right now, but you are in danger from my own family. Please leave Lakes Entrance and head for Melbourne. I will bring your bags as soon as it is safe. I love you. C U Soon. My mate, my heart. 🩶

My breath stops.

Danger. From his family.

This can't be a joke.

This can't be some overprotective mate-bond paranoia. Deep down, I know it's real. Braven's message is serious.

Deadly serious.

I look around me, at the different vehicles parked in the car park, suddenly aware of every shadow.

I'm pregnant. I'm alone. And now I'm being hunted.

Oh shit.

And the doctor basically confirmed I'm walking around with a target on my back.

What the hell has Braven dragged me into? Or worse — what do they know about my blood work?

What did those tests reveal?

My stomach twists as I shove my phone back into my pocket and scan the car park. Relief washes through me when I don't see anyone lurking in the shadows.

Good.

One thing going right.

I dig through my handbag, fingers brushing past receipts, lip gloss, and my pregnancy test before finding my keys. I unlock the car and take a slow, deliberate walk around it.

The whole thing is coated in dust, grime and salt sea air — four days of sitting untouched — but I don't have time to care.

Tyres: inflated.

Windows: intact.

No smashed glass or panels.

No slashed rubber.

So far, so good.

But something in my gut whispers, Check again.

I crouch down and sweep my hand along the underside of the car. My fingers brush something small, hard, and out of place.

What the hell?

I pull it free — a dark, unfamiliar object, cold and metallic. My instincts flare. I grab my phone, snap a picture, and place the object on the tyre of a nearby car.

Then I drop to my knees and slide my phone under my car, recording video as I sweep the camera across the undercarriage.

A minute later, I stand and replay the footage. There. Another one. Wedged near the drive shaft.

I drop down again, heart pounding, and reach under. Not one — two. Both jammed in tight. I yank them free with more force than I expect and snap another photo before tossing all three objects into the industrial rubbish bin.

Whatever they are, I don't want them anywhere near me.

I open the passenger door, grab the packet of wet wipes from the glove compartment, and scrub my hands clean. Something in my head screams, *'Don't throw the wipes away.'* So I drop them onto the floor of the car instead and tuck the packet back into the glove box.

I shut the door, lock it, and circle around to the driver's side. I hit the unlock button once — only my door. No one else is getting in.

I glance around again. Still clear. Still alone.

I slide into the driver's seat, slam the door shut, and lock it immediately. My handbag hits the passenger seat. My phone clicks into its cradle and begins charging.

Fuel gauge: enough to get me to Bairnsdale.

Plan: fill up there, grab food, then drive straight to Melbourne.

Braven said to leave. So I'm leaving.

I start the engine. The car rumbles to life.

My pulse thunders in my ears. I grip the steering wheel, take one steadying breath, and whisper to myself: "Okay, Misty. Time to go."

Because whatever is happening here — wolves, blood tests, kill orders, Braven's family — I'm not sticking around to find out the hard way.

CHAPTER TWENTY-THREE
BRAVEN

I DO NOT HAVE TO SEE THE MESSAGE ON MY PHONE TO know Misty has left Lakes Entrance.

I feel it.

A subtle shift in the bond — faint, incomplete, but unmistakable. A tug in my chest. A hollowing in my gut. A sense of distance that shouldn't exist. My mate is leaving the territory.

My cat prowls inside me, restless and agitated, pacing the confines of my skin. He wants out. He wants to chase her. He wants to drag her back to safety. He wants to protect her — our mate, our future, our cub.

I think it is time.

I have to find out how to release her cat.

Because whatever happened to Misty as a child — whatever blocked her animal, whatever sealed away her instincts — it's preventing her from shifting. Preventing her from feeling the full bond. Preventing her from sensing me the way I sense her.

If only she knew how to shift. If only she had grown up knowing what she is. If only she had been allowed to be who she was born to be.

In the short time I've spent with her, the bond we do share is growing, strengthening, weaving itself through my soul like it's reclaiming old territory. But the sad truth is... right now, it's only a one-way bond.

She can't feel me. Not fully. Not the way I feel her.

If only it were safe enough for Misty to release her cat and shift — then she would feel everything. Our mated bond. Our soulmate bond. My love for her.

I enter my house through the internal garage door and lift my nose to the air. My senses flare, scanning for intruders, for unfamiliar scents, for anything out of place. With everything happening, I can't take chances. Not with Misty's life on the line. Not with wolves sniffing around. Not with my father scheming.

The house smells clean. Untouched. Safe — for now.

With a quick tap on my phone screen, I open the message Misty sent earlier.

MISTY:

> Doctors apptmt is finished. All went well. Had a few bugs stuck on my car. All clean now. I'll c u soon.

A smile pulls at my lips. She picked up her car. She's on her way back to Melbourne. She's out of Lakes Entrance. Relief floods me. Hang on...what bugs? With everything happening, with my family and the rogue wolves, she couldn't possibly be speaking of trackers on her car?

How would she know to look for them in the first place? At the moment, I don't care. Goes to show my mate is resourceful.

Approaching my bedroom, I pack my bags quickly, grabbing Misty's belongings as well. I return to the garage and load everything into the boot of my car. I strip off my clothes, shove the soiled ones into a plastic bag, and toss it into the boot with the rest.

I move through the house with purpose — resetting the security alarm, locking windows, checking that no documents or files are left out. Every movement is automatic, practiced, efficient.

But something inside me is pushing. Hard. A deep instinctive warning. A primal urgency. Danger is coming.

I grab my jacket, wallet, keys, and phone. I lock every door behind me before stepping back into the garage. I climb into my car, press the button to open the roller door, and start the engine.

The moment there's enough clearance, I hit the accelerator. The car shoots backward out of the garage.

Once clear, I hit the remote near the sun visor, closing the garage door. I spin the car around, shift into drive, and take off down the long gravel driveway. My tyres spit dust behind me as I race toward the main road.

A glance in the rear-view mirror freezes my blood. Two panthers — massive, black, powerful — sprint to a stop near my house. My father's enforcers.

A breath escapes me — half relief, half fury. That was far too close.

I force myself to focus on the road, scanning the mirrors,

checking the tree line, watching for movement. I can't afford to be followed. Not now. Not when Misty is alone.

Just before entering the township of Lakes Entrance, I grab my phone and switch it off. If my father is tracking me — and he will be — I can't risk him tracing my movements.

First stop: fuel.

If my credit cards start being monitored, I need a full tank before I disappear. If anyone sees me in town and reports back to my father, he'll assume I'm picking up Misty from the doctor's.

Good.

Let him think that.

I'll take the back roads out of Lakes Entrance — the ones only locals know. I'll detour through the bush tracks, cross the old logging route, and rejoin the highway miles away from where anyone expects.

I need a head start. A big one.

Thankfully, I memorised Misty's driver's licence — her address, her suburb, her building. I'll drive there first. I'll wait for her. I'll make sure she arrives safely.

It's going to be a long drive. Hours of distance between us. Hours of not knowing if she's safe. And my heart already aches — physically aches — to be with my soulmate again.

My Misty.

CHAPTER TWENTY-FOUR
MISTY

WITH JUST UNDER FOUR HOURS OF STRESSFUL driving, I finally pull into my apartment building. My shoulders ache, my eyes burn, and my nerves feel like they've been scraped raw. I decide to park in my brand-new parking spot — compliments of my brand-new apartment — the one I officially own.

With everything going on, it feels safer having my car in a different position in the multi-storey carpark. Different floor. Different location. Different angle.

No one should find my car here in a hurry.

Still... I'm not ready to be alone. Not after today. Not after the doctor. Not after Braven's message. Not after the trackers under my car.

I need someone who grounds me.

Someone who knows me.

Someone who won't think I'm insane.

LJ.

With only my handbag for luggage, I make my way to the seventh floor and ring the doorbell. Even though I have a key, this is not the time to just barge in. What if she has a guy over?

Oh Gods. I should have called first. I sigh, shaking my head. I just hope LJ forgives me for this intrusion.

Then something strange happens. I sense her. Not hear with my ears. Not see with my eyes. Not imagine with my imagination. Sense.

A presence moving toward the door. A familiar warmth. A flicker of recognition in my chest. It's subtle, but it's there — like a new instinct waking up.

My foot taps nervously against the carpet as I wait. Within seconds, the sound of LJ fiddling with the locks reaches my ears — sharper than usual, clearer, like my senses have been dialled up.

Another thing to add to my *"new sensations"* basket.

The door swings open, revealing a very surprised LJ. Before I can breathe, she engulfs me in one of her signature hugs — warm, tight, grounding. Gods, I needed this. I feel it all the way to my heart.

She pulls me inside, shutting the door with a soft click. Her hands clasp mine, warm against my cold fingers. She steps back, eyes scanning my face like she's reading every thought I've ever had.

"Oh, my gawd. Look at you. There is something very different about you. I can see it. But hang on. What are you doing here? I thought you'd still have a few days left in Lakes Entrance? What happened?"

Her hands tighten around mine. "Misty, what has happened?"

I force a breath into my lungs and meet her gaze. My lips try to form a smile, but it probably looks more like a grimace. I tug gently on her hands and pull her toward the kitchen.

"Come on, let's make a cuppa. It's been a long drive. While the kettle is boiling, I'll go to the loo, and when I come back, we'll sit down, and I'll explain what's been happening. You're going to think I've gone crazy."

Concern spreads across her face, but she nods and releases my hands, turning toward the kitchen.

Okay. She's worried. And she should be.

My eyes drift to the tiled stone-coloured floor beneath my shoes. My mind spins. How do I even begin? How do I say the words out loud?

"Hey LJ, turns out I've been married to my childhood soulmate all my life. And guess what? I'm a cat shifter. Oh, and I'm pregnant."

Yeah. LJ is really going to be—

"What?"

LJ's voice screeches through the apartment.

I jump so high I swear I clear the floor by a foot. Pain shoots through my knees and ankles when I land.

I stare at her. She's facing me now, hand over her heart, the other covering her open mouth. Shock radiates off her.

What just happened?

Why is she looking at me like that?

She had her back to me — how did she hear—

"Misty, what did you just say?"

Huh?

I blink. Did I... did I say all that out loud? Oh. Shit.

"LJ, what was the last thing I said?"

"Misty, what do you mean you are mated to your childhood soulmate?"

Oh shit.

I did say it out loud.

Not how I planned. Not even close.

With a tiny, awkward smile, I whisper, "Surprise."

LJ stares at me, eyes wide, brain clearly firing at a million miles an hour.

"For fuck sake, Misty. I knew you didn't know about your shifter side. I've seen your mating bite. I figured your mate had died, or you had no memory of your old life. Or something."

Wait.

What?

LJ already knew I was a shifter?

She looks away, eyes dropping to the floor. Hiding something. Avoiding something.

"LJ," I say slowly, "how did you know I'm meant to be a shifter when I had no idea? I still don't know if I can shift. I'm only going by what Braven and the doctor told me."

"Is Braven your soulmate?"

Ooh. She's quick. "Yes, LJ. Braven O'Geary is my childhood soulmate. He's also my client in Lakes Entrance."

"You have to be shitting me. You met with a local clan of shifters and didn't know what they were?"

I roll my eyes. "No, LJ. I've only met Braven and the doctor. Well... on my first day, I did have a run-in with three wolf shifters. They wanted me to go with them to speak to their boss. I ended up fighting two of the stupid wolves."

"You what?" LJ screams. "Oh, man. What else have you been up to, apart from having lots of sex with your soulmate?"

Heat crawls up my neck. "I don't remember much of the marathon sex session because I was in heat. A lot of it is a blur. But I do remember some parts where Braven turned into a large black cat a few times."

"You were in heat, and now you're pregnant with your soulmate. Oh, wow. What did Braven say when you saw him again after all those years? Did he recognise you?"

"Look, LJ. I'm going to the bathroom. You're going to make our drinks. We will discuss all things shifters as soon as I empty my annoying bladder."

I FEEL LOST AS I LOOK OVER THE CITY, THE LIGHTS blurring into streaks through the balcony glass. My mind is still spinning, still trying to process everything LJ just told me. I expected her not to believe me — expected laughter, disbelief, maybe even concern for my mental health — but instead she dropped a bombshell of her own.

She knows about the paranormal.

Witches.

Shifters.

Different species.

Different clans.

She knows more than I do. And that alone is enough to make my stomach twist.

Still feeling like LJ is hiding something, I demanded she tell me the truth. She's meant to be my best friend — my sister in everything but blood — yet she's been sitting on information that changes my entire life.

With guilt eating her alive and with tears in her eyes, LJ finally confessed. Her parents had been friends with my parents.

The words hit me like a punch to the chest. I sit there, stunned, unable to move, unable to breathe.

I listen as LJ explains how her parents were approached by mine — desperate, terrified — and asked to perform some kind of spell. A spell to prevent me from shifting. A spell to keep the entire paranormal world hidden from me.

The cost?

My memories.

Everything before eight years old. Everything about my childhood. Everything about my soulmate.

It turns out I had become extremely sick being away from Braven. My parents became desperate because if I had stayed on that path, I would have slowly died.

I stare at the tall glass in my hand — ice, coke, and rum — and watch the ice cubes tinkle against one another. I didn't realise how badly I needed the drink until the smooth liquid slid down my parched throat. The condensation drips slowly down the side of the glass, and I automatically take another sip. Then another. Until an ice cube slips into my mouth.

I crunch it between my teeth, the cold shocking me back into my body.

Then it hits me.

I'm pregnant.

I shouldn't be drinking.

Oh, SHIT.

The baby — the blob.

I quickly place the half-full glass on the coffee table and look up at LJ.

"Um. Thank you for the drink, but I had better stick with water, juice, and tea."

"Why? Is there something wrong with your drink?"

I shake my head. "No. It's lovely. But now that I'm pregnant, I should keep clear of alcohol."

Her eyes widen. She leans forward, gaze dropping to my flat belly.

"Shit. Misty. I forgot about the no alcohol for a pregnant woman. Sorry. But that is going to suck big time."

I nod, pick up the glass, and offer it to her. "Tell me about it. Here, you might as well finish mine. No point letting it go to waste."

LJ smiles and takes the glass, lifting it to her lips. My mouth waters as I watch her throat move with each swallow. Gods, I hope I made the right decision letting her finish it. But this pregnancy — if I continue with it — I want to do the right thing for the little blob.

My blob.

I smile, thinking back to today's ultrasound. Seeing that tiny grainy dot for the first time. The blob my so-called specialists said I would never be able to have. Which reminds me — I'll need to make an appointment with one of them tomorrow.

LJ's voice pulls me back. "What has you smiling like a love-struck girl?"

I glance at her, warmth blooming in my chest. I can tell her anything.

"I had an ultrasound today," I murmur. "I got to see my

little Blob." My hand drifts to my belly, resting there instinctively.

LJ practically launches herself across the couch, nearly landing in my lap, excitement lighting up her eyes. "You really are pregnant? You're going to have a little baby. Did you get a picture?"

I reach for my phone, swipe across the screen, and open the text message from the doctor. He'd taken several photos of the scan — proof that the blob is real. Proof that something impossible is happening inside me.

I hand her the phone and watch her face transform — confusion, curiosity, then pure joy as she realises what she's looking at.

That tiny blob is my baby.

My baby.

My Blob.

Tears fill her eyes, and I can see the love she has for me — the pride, the joy, the disbelief. We've known each other for so many years; we're more like sisters than friends.

Seeing that love reflected back at me sets off my own waterworks.

Shit.

This is all I need — to become a watering pot.

"Oh my gawd, Misty," LJ whispers, cries, her voice trembling. "This little dot is your baby, isn't it?"

Chapter Twenty-Five
Misty

AFTER THREE HOURS OF SLEEP CURLED UP ON THIS super-soft queen-size bed, my head resting among four matching feather pillows, my body attempts to stretch. A long, slow, feline-like stretch that pulls at my muscles and makes me want to sink back into the warmth.

Why am I even contemplating waking? What has my mind on alert? Something keeps niggling at me. A tug. A whisper. A pressure behind my ribs. I've been holding off from texting Braven, but now I wonder if he's okay. Where he might be. What he meant when he said I was in danger. What kind of danger?

LJ intrudes on my thoughts — the conversation we had earlier replaying in my mind. I feel relieved after explaining everything to her. Relieved she believed me. Relieved she didn't think I'd lost my mind.

LJ agreed wholeheartedly for me to stay with her tonight.

Somehow, I have the feeling it's more about her keeping an eye on me. And honestly? I'm grateful.

LJ filled me in on her history — what she is, who her parents were, and what they did for mine.

Wow. I still cannot believe my best friend is a witch and a cat shifter.

I wonder if she'll be able to help me find a way to shift. The doctor said I should avoid shifting for a couple of days. If I'm careful, I can attempt it after that. He also mentioned it's not advisable to shift after five months — not for the baby, and not for me.

My hand drifts across my lower belly in light strokes. My mind drifts to my parents. I wonder what they would have thought of all this. Would they have arranged a meeting with Braven before now? Would they have told me the truth?

It would be good to know the real reason they took off, went into hiding, and changed my identity.

A keen sense to get up hits me — sharp, sudden, insistent. I think of Braven. I feel as if I should go to my apartment. Something is not right. I can feel it.

I quietly move from LJ's guest bedroom. My bare feet lift quickly off the cold tiled floor with each step I take. I make my way toward the kitchen for a drink of water — my lips dry, my throat parched. I should have taken a glass earlier before falling asleep.

A loud shriek tears out of me as my feet leave the floor. My heart nearly bursts out of my chest. My body almost jumps out of my skin when LJ appears beside me.

"Hey. What are you doing?" LJ says. My hands clutch my

chest, feeling my heart galloping like it's trying to escape. "Shit. Are you okay? Sorry, Misty, I thought you noticed me."

I try to gulp air into my lungs — attempted breaths not helping. My heart continues to race, thumping painfully against my ribs.

"Geez, LJ," I wheeze, "No, I am not okay. Shit. Girl, warn a person next time."

LJ places her hand against my back. The awareness of her touch brings me back to Earth. Her body heat penetrates through the thin material of the t-shirt I'm wearing. I know she's trying to help. But right now, I can't handle her touching me.

Something is happening. Something inside me. Something pushing, urging, warning. I need my own clothes back on. I need to check my apartment. I need to move.

I sense it again — that pull. That pressure. That instinct.

Braven.

He's close.

With effort, I move away from LJ and her scorching touch.

"Misty. Talk to me. What is going through your mind?"

A small sarcastic laugh escapes me. "LJ, there are a lot of things racing through my mind. Braven is one of the main items moving to the front. Something is pushing me to go. I think he has arrived here at the apartment complex."

I walk back into the guest bedroom and reach for the long black leggings folded on the chest of drawers. It doesn't take long before I'm pulling them up over my hips, watching my toes slip through the ends.

I should be thankful to LJ for the clothes she left for me —

especially since she put mine in the wash so I'd have something clean to wear in the morning.

"Misty, don't go anywhere without me. I am coming with you. Wait back in the lounge room while I get dressed."

I nod quickly, slip one of her knitted jumpers over my head, and push my hands through the sleeves. The more seconds pass, the stronger the feeling gets.

Braven is here. He's nearby. And he's in trouble.

I slide my thick-socked feet into my shoes and return to the lounge room. LJ appears moments later, dressed and ready.

I grab my apartment keys from the kitchen bench. LJ does the same — and reaches for her mobile phone and something brown and green.

Is that a branch?

I blink. Shake my head. Tell myself LJ knows what she's doing.

We step out of her front door and head toward my floor — toward my apartment — toward whatever is waiting for us.

I just hope we run into Braven... and not anyone else.

CHAPTER TWENTY-SIX
BRAVEN

NOW I REMEMBER WHY I DO NOT ENJOY TRAVELLING to the city. I hate it here. Far too many vehicles. Far too many people. And the smell — exhaust fumes, hot concrete, stale food, too many bodies in too small a space. How do people stand it?

I carefully manoeuvre my car around the endless stream of other cars, weaving through traffic like I'm navigating a battlefield. I swear I'll end up with grey hair after this.

Finally, I spot a sign on my left. Relief hits me like a wave. I've nearly arrived at Misty's apartment complex.

But then — a strange sensation crawls up my spine. A warning. A whisper. A push. Something encourages me to drive past the turn-off and circle the block. Why do I have the feeling someone is watching me?

My eyes flick to the mirrors, scanning the street, the footpaths, the rooftops. Nothing obvious. But my instincts don't lie. My cat doesn't lie.

I circle the block once, twice, then approach the complex again. This time, I turn sharply into the dark entrance of the carpark and follow close behind another vehicle. The boom gate begins to lower, but the car in front slows just enough for me to slip through before it shuts.

Lucky.

Reading the signs and following the arrows, I park my car where Misty should have parked hers. Her allocated spot. Her brand-new apartment. Her brand-new life.

But her car isn't here.

Hmm. This is strange. Where is Misty's car?

I step out of my vehicle, my nose lifting instinctively. I inhale deeply — searching for her scent. Nothing. Not fresh. Not recent. Not even lingering.

Damn. Where is she? Is she safe?

My nerves tighten. Something is wrong. I can feel it — a pressure in my chest, a warning in my bones.

I grab our bags from the car and head for her floor, moving quickly, silently. When I reach her apartment, I pull out the spare key I had made when she was staying at my house.

She's going to be pissed when she finds out. But I don't care. I need to know she's safe. I unlock the door and step inside.

Misty's scent hits me — sweet, warm, familiar — but faint. Old. Days old. She hasn't been back here yet. Now I'm really starting to worry.

I check every room, every corner, every shadow. Nothing. No sign of her. No sign of a struggle. No sign of anyone else.

I return to the main living area and turn off the lights, letting the darkness settle around me. Misty lives in a beautiful, modern apartment — clean lines, soft colours, her scent woven into the space like a whisper.

My ears twitch. Someone is at the door.

Shit. I freeze, listening. A scrape of metal against the lock.

Whoever it is — they have a key.

I slip into the shadows, pressing my back against the wall, ready to strike. My muscles coil, my cat pushing forward, claws itching beneath my skin.

The door opens slowly. "Braven, are you here?"

My breath escapes in a rush. My heart stops — then slams back into motion.

Misty. Thank God.

I step out of the shadows and into the dim hallway light.

My eyes drink her in — my beautiful soulmate, alive, safe, glowing with something I can't name. My hands twitch at my sides. I want to grab her, hold her, bury my face in her neck and breathe her in.

Knowing she's safe. Knowing our baby is safe.

"Oh, thank fuck," Misty says, reaching down to grab her laptop bag. "Braven, quick. Grab the bags and follow me. We cannot stay here. Something is not right. We have to go."

My mind shuts down — overwhelmed by the sight of her — but my body moves on autopilot. I grab the bags as she instructed.

Then my nose catches something. Misty is not alone.

I lift my head and see a strange woman standing in the doorway. Her eyes assess me quickly before darting down the corridor. She's alert. Focused. Dangerous.

Who the fuck is this woman with my mate? My senses scream at me — move now, ask questions later.

We exit the apartment, and I follow close behind Misty. Over my shoulder, I see the strange woman waving something in front of the door. A branch. A literal branch. Whatever she's doing makes my nose twitch — like the air is shifting, clearing, changing.

Danger presses in around us. Something is approaching. Something wrong.

I focus on Misty's sexy arse and keep walking — because if I don't, I'll lose my mind.

We reach the elevator. The doors begin to close — but the strange woman rushes in at the last second, still waving her stick.

What the...?

Is that a branch of a tree?

Misty breaks the silence. "Um. LJ. What are you doing exactly?"

After another dramatic arm wave, the woman — LJ — finally answers.

"Misty, if you really need to know, I am clearing and removing your scent, and now your friend's scent, from the building."

Huh.

Wow.

Really?

This woman — LJ — is starting to spin me out.

"I can feel there are other shifters in the complex," LJ continues, tilting her head like she's listening to something only she can hear. "Shifters who seem... I'm not sure if evil is the right word, but I am sensing these shifters mean you harm."

My mouth opens — then closes slowly. My eyes dart to Misty's shocked face.

"Holy shit, LJ, you can really do that? Remove our scent so no one will know we were even here?" Misty asks, awe in her voice.

With a smug look, LJ nods. "Yep. Sure can. Cool, hey."

Misty breathes, "Wow. LJ. That is cool."

The elevator hums around us. The air thickens. Danger presses closer. And I know — without a doubt — we are running out of time.

With a ding, the elevator doors quietly open.

For a moment, I swear Misty and LJ forget I'm even here. I shake my head slightly and wait for Misty to step through the open doors.

All three of us exit — Misty in front, me behind her, LJ trailing us while waving that damn branch around like she's conducting an orchestra of spirits. If my hands weren't full of bags, I'd rub my twitching nose. Whatever enchantment she's doing, it smells sharp and earthy, like crushed leaves and lightning.

We pass two closed doors before Misty stops at the third. She unlocks it with a soft click and pushes it open.

We step into a bright, modern apartment — open, stylish, expensive. Whoever decorated this place knew what they were doing. Clean lines. Soft tones. Everything curated.

Very different from Misty's apartment — though, to be fair, I wasn't exactly paying attention to décor when I was searching for my mate.

The door closes behind us with a snick. I glance back to see

LJ smiling at me — slowly, deliberately — her eyes sweeping over me in a way that makes my cat bristle.

Uh-oh.

I know that look.

Assessment. Curiosity. A hint of mischief.

Before I can react, Misty's voice pulls me back.

"Braven, you can place my things in the guest bedroom... This way."

My head snaps toward her. My mate. My focus. My everything.

I follow her down the hall, glancing back once to see LJ wink at me.

"Don't worry," she says lightly. "We weren't followed." Then, with a knowing smirk: "Go. You don't need my permission. Better hurry up and follow her."

I don't need to be told twice. I step into the guest bedroom, Misty's scent wrapping around me like a warm hand. My chest tightens. My heart aches. I drop the bags by the bed, scanning the room.

Where did she go? The sound of running water reaches my ears — soft, steady, unmistakable. A shower.

My pulse jumps. I move toward the sound, pausing at the bathroom doorway. Steam curls out, warm and inviting. I hesitate — not because I don't want her, but because I want to respect her space.

But the bond... The pull... The need to see her, touch her, reassure myself she's safe... It's overwhelming.

I close the bedroom door quietly, locking it. My jacket comes off. My shirt follows. My shoes hit the floor. Next the rest of my clothing.

I step into the bathroom. And there she is. My mate. My wife. My pregnant soulmate.

Standing beneath the hot spray, steam swirling around her like a veil. Water glides over her skin, tracing every curve, every line, every place I've memorised and missed.

My breath catches. My chest tightens. My cat pushes forward, desperate to claim, to protect, to hold.

I move toward her — slow, reverent — letting the moment settle around us. My hands find her waist, her belly, her shoulders. She leans back into me instinctively, like her body recognises mine before her mind does.

Her scent hits me — warm, sweet, uniquely hers — and something inside me settles for the first time since I left her.

I press my forehead to her shoulder, breathing her in.

"Misty…"

Her name leaves me like a prayer. She turns her head slightly, giving me access to her neck. My lips brush her skin — soft, warm, familiar — and she shivers.

The bond flares. Not fully. Not completely. But enough. Enough to feel her relief. Her exhaustion. Her fear. Her need. Enough to know she's been holding herself together by sheer force of will.

I wrap my arms around her, pulling her back against my chest, shielding her from everything — the world, the danger, the wolves, my father, fate itself.

"I've got you," I murmur against her skin. "I'm here."

She exhales — a soft, trembling sound — and her hands come up to rest over mine. For a long moment, we just stand there.

Water. Steam. Breathing one another in. Feeling the Bond. Two souls finally in the same place again.

When she turns in my arms, her eyes meet mine — wide, vulnerable, fierce, and full of something that makes my chest ache.

Love. Recognition. Home.

She reaches up, touches my cheek, and whispers, "Braven..."

I kiss her — slow, deep, claiming and claimed — the kind of kiss that says everything we don't have words for yet.

The kind of kiss that says: You're mine. I'm yours. We survived today. We'll survive tomorrow. Together.

When we finally break apart, breathless and pressed close, I rest my forehead against hers. "I love you," I whisper. "More than you know."

Her fingers curl into my shoulders. Her lips brush mine again. And the bond hums between us — warm, alive, growing. And with it, we make slow passionate love against the wall tiles, under the warm waterspray.

My mate. My heart. My future.

CHAPTER TWENTY-SEVEN
MISTY

BRAVEN'S FINGERS GLIDE OVER MY SKIN LIKE HE'S memorising me, slow and reverent, as if rinsing away the evidence of what we just did is some kind of sacred ritual. The steam curls around us, thick and warm, but I'm shivering anyway. Not from cold. From him. From everything that's suddenly too big to hold inside my chest.

His body slips from mine, his thumb sweeps along the inside of my thigh, and my breath stutters. I'm supposed to be forming sentences — real ones, important ones — but my brain is still melted somewhere between his hands and the wall behind me. Every time he touches me, another thought slips through my fingers.

Braven's hands move over me with a focus that steals the air from my lungs. He isn't rushing. He isn't distracted. He's touching me like he's grounding himself, like he's making sure I'm really here with him and not slipping away again. Warm water trails down my skin, carrying the last remnants of what we just shared, but his palms stay firm, steady, almost reverent.

I should speak. I should pull the words out of my throat and tell him everything. But every time his fingers skim another inch of me, my thoughts dissolve into the steam curling around us.

"We need to talk," I manage, though it sounds more like a breath than a sentence.

Braven pauses — not stopping, just... listening. His gaze lifts to mine, dark and intense, like he's bracing for something he can't name yet. His thumb strokes my hip once, slow, reassuring.

"I know," he says quietly. "I'm not going anywhere."

That simple promise hits harder than it should. My chest tightens. My hand finds his shoulder, needing the anchor, needing him close because the truth inside me feels too big to hold alone.

The scan. Blob. The tiny shape on that screen that changed everything the moment I saw it.

My stomach twists, not with fear this time, but with the weight of what comes next.

"Braven..." His name slips out, shaky. "There's something I need to show you."

His whole body stills. Not tense — alert. Present. His eyes search mine, and I can see the moment he senses the shift, the seriousness threading through my voice.

He steps closer, water running between us, his forehead brushing mine. "Tell me."

I swallow hard. My fingers tremble where they rest against his skin. "I went to the clinic. Before all of this. I... I had a scan."

A breath catches in his chest.

I press my palm over my lower stomach, the memory of that grainy little shape flashing behind my eyes. "You haven't seen it yet. But you need to. You need to meet Blob."

Confusion flickers across his face — then something else. Something fierce and soft all at once.

He lifts his hand, covering mine where it rests against my belly, his touch gentle in a way that makes my throat burn.

"Misty," he murmurs, voice low, roughened by emotion he hasn't named yet.

The water keeps falling. The steam keeps rising. But the world narrows to this — his hand over mine, the truth between us, and the tiny life waiting to be acknowledged.

And for the first time since I saw that scan, I don't feel alone.

CHAPTER TWENTY-EIGHT
BRAVEN

FULLY DRESSED AND SITTING BACK OUT IN THE LARGE, spacious lounge room, I settle into one of the three four-seater lounge chairs arranged around LJ's glass-top, teak-stained coffee table. I make sure I sit on the same seat Misty chose, leaving her space, even though my thigh keeps drifting, brushing hers. Every accidental-on-purpose touch sends a low thrum up my side, like my body is reminding me exactly who she is to me.

LJ places three steaming mugs on the table before dropping into the seat opposite us. Her gaze flicks between us, sharp and amused.

"Okay, folks. I think it's time we all have a little chat. First, welcome to my home, Braven." She smiles at me like she already knows I'm about to make this awkward.

Something nudges my leg. Misty. Again. I take the hint.

"Um. Hi, LJ." Smooth. Real smooth. "Thank you for being here for Misty. I'm relieved she has someone looking out for her."

One of LJ's eyebrows climbs her forehead like it's trying to escape. Perfect. I'm absolutely nailing this. NOT.

"Look, LJ," I try again, clearing my throat. "All I'm trying to say is... thanks for looking out for Misty. From what I've seen, you care about each other a lot. And thank you for letting me into your home."

LJ's expression softens, her smile warming. "Aww, Braven. See? That wasn't so hard. Now that you've tripped over your words enough, I think it's time you fill us in on why you're here — and who the shifters are roaming my building."

Direct. Good. I can work with direct.

"Okay." I nod. "As you know, my name is Braven O'Geary. I'm the eldest son of my alpha. The Lakes Entrance Black Panther Pack. My job is to one day take over the clan from my bastard of a father. I don't trust my family or my clan right now."

Two simultaneous gasps hit me — Misty's and LJ's. Their eyes stay locked on me, waiting.

"Today, my father wanted to meet Misty. After a few brief words with him, it became clear he was up to something. Something aimed at Misty." I turn to her, meeting those eyes that undo me every time. "That's why I texted you. Why I told you to leave town. Not long after I got home and packed our bags, I sensed clan members approaching my house. When I drove out of the garage, several cats came out of the woods. I barely escaped."

I look between them, trying to read both faces at once.

"I realised my father would assume I'd pick Misty up from the doctor's. I told him she's my soulmate and was having the pregnancy confirmed."

"You did what?" Misty's voice spikes, sharp enough to cut. Her eyes flash, and my stomach drops. Great. Annoyed already. Fantastic start.

"Misty," I say carefully, "my father was pushing me to get back with my ex, Liasa. He was furious I went to the elders instead of him to annul the mating. He's a bastard, so I told him the truth — that I have someone else. That we've mated. That you're my soulmate. And that you're expecting our first child."

LJ inhales sharply. "Oh shit. That's why they're here. They're after both of you. Braven, you've put Misty in more danger than you realise."

My head snaps toward her. "How? Misty's in the city. More places to hide. And that little stick you've been waving around seems to be keeping them away."

"For now," LJ says. "But it won't hold forever. Especially once Misty goes back to work."

My head whips back to Misty. "You're going back to work?"

She gives me a look that could peel paint. "Braven, we might be mated soulmates and pregnant, but that doesn't give you the right to tell me how to live. Yes, I'm going back to work. I'm good at my job. And tomorrow, I have an appointment with my specialist about the pregnancy."

My pulse stutters. "What are you saying, Misty?"

"I'm living in Melbourne," she says, steady and sure. "I need a doctor here. LJ assures me my specialist deals with shifters."

LJ cuts in before I can respond. "Speaking of shifting — Misty, you should stay here and use my safe room. We need to practice your shifting and figure out how to break this blocking spell."

Blocking spell?

"Huh? Blocking spell?" My voice comes out louder than intended. "What are you talking about?"

"Well, genius," LJ says dryly, "our girl here has a spell on her. It's preventing her from shifting."

I stare at Misty, stunned. "You know it's a spell? You're sure?"

"Yes," LJ says. "I'm sure."

"How?" I demand.

"Because my aunt is the one who placed it on her. Years ago. I just need to figure out exactly what she did so I can undo it."

The room tilts. "What? You know who did this to Misty?"

"Braven," LJ says, gentler now, "Misty's parents were desperate to keep her alive. This was the only way they knew."

My jaw clenches. My hands curl into fists. My pulse roars in my ears. Misty. Spellbound. Trapped in her own skin. And her parents did it to save her.

The world narrows to a single, burning truth: Someone stole her birthright. And I'm going to get it back if it's the last thing I do.

CHAPTER TWENTY-NINE
MISTY

AFTER LAST NIGHT'S ENTERTAINMENT — BRAVEN AND LJ firing questions at each other like they're in some supernatural courtroom — I'd given up trying to referee. The back-and-forth had set the tiny hairs on my neck on edge, and I'd crawled into bed before either of them could drag me into round two. I knew Braven would follow. He always does.

Now I'm in LJ's kitchen, hunched over my tea, fully dressed and ready to go. Morning light spills through her windows, soft and golden, but my stomach is a tight knot. My specialist appointment looms in my mind like a storm cloud.

IT HITS ME NOW — WHY LJ INSISTED ON THIS particular specialist. Why she practically shoved the appointment card into my hand. The fertility specialist deals with shifters. Actual shifters. Apparently, the city is crawling with them, working normal jobs, blending in like it's no big deal.

When I think back to the strange questions he asked me two months ago, the ones that made no sense at the time... yeah. Only a shifter would've known what he was hinting at.

And then the internal exam. The moment he would've seen the mark on my inner thigh — the one Braven recognised instantly, the one I didn't understand at all. No mate present. Virginity intact. No answers. No knowledge of shifters. Of course he assumed I was infertile. Of course he thought I had no mate. He wasn't wrong. Not then.

This whole paranormal world has been sitting under my nose my entire life, and I've been blissfully ignorant. Hidden truths wrapped in romance novels I thought were pure fantasy. Turns out they weren't lying. Shifters are real. And I'm one of them.

Now I'm back in the same office, LJ on one side, Braven on the other. His hand squeezes mine every few seconds, like he's trying to keep his nerves from leaking out through his leg. It's bouncing. Hard. The chair is practically vibrating. I take a slow breath and wait.

"Mrs O'Geary?"

My head snaps up. Not my name. Someone else's. I grit my teeth. Braven's leg stops shaking. I turn toward him just as he starts to stand.

"Yes. Over here," he calls, far too enthusiastically.

What the hell?

My gaze darts around the room. O'Geary. That's his surname. Maybe his mother is here? His sister? Someone else entirely?

Then his grip tightens around my hand, dragging my attention back to him. "Baby, they're calling for you."

No. Absolutely not. My name is not O'Geary.

"Misty," he says, like he's explaining something obvious to a toddler, "because we're mates, in our society we're classed as husband and wife. We're mated."

My eyes widen. Then narrow. Oh, hell no.

Braven must see the storm brewing because he releases my hand like it's suddenly on fire.

The nurse calls again — "Mrs O'Geary?" — and I sigh, long and suffering. Time to stand.

I grab my bag. A giggle snags my attention. LJ. Of course. Her grin says everything. I shoot her a look that translates perfectly to *don't you dare*.

She giggles again anyway, then steps beside me with a straight face she absolutely does not deserve. "Come on, Mrs O'Geary," she says. "Let's get this over with."

I exhale, square my shoulders, and walk toward the nurse calling me a name I never agreed to.

But Braven's eyes follow me like I already belong to it.

AFTER A ROUND OF TESTS, FOLLOWED BY AN ultrasound, we're escorted into yet another private office. Another room. Another set of chairs. Another stretch of waiting for someone in a white coat to appear and tell me what's happening inside my own body.

I drop into the nearest seat with a sigh. If this is the precedent for my pregnancy, I'm in trouble. Endless waiting rooms. Endless fluorescent lighting. Endless strangers calling me Mrs O'Geary like that's a perfectly normal thing to do.

Braven sits beside me, close enough that his knee brushes mine every few seconds. He's trying to look calm, but his leg keeps bouncing, betraying him. LJ leans against the wall, arms folded, eyes flicking between us like she's watching a live-action soap opera she didn't realise she'd been cast in.

The room smells faintly of disinfectant and stale air-conditioning. A soft hum buzzes from the vent overhead. My fingers tap against my thigh, restless. My mind keeps replaying the ultrasound — the grainy little shape on the screen, the tiny flicker that made my breath catch.

Blob.

My chest tightens. I'm not sure if it's nerves or awe or the creeping realisation that everything in my life has shifted without asking my permission.

Braven's hand slides over mine, warm and steady. His thumb strokes once, slow. I don't look at him, but I feel the weight of his gaze on the side of my face.

LJ clears her throat, breaking the silence. "You two look like you're waiting for a verdict."

She's not wrong. I lean back in the chair, exhaling through my nose. "Feels like it."

Braven's fingers tighten around mine, just a fraction. Protective. Nervous. Hopeful. All of it bleeding through his touch.

The door handle clicks. All three of us straighten at once. My heart thuds against my ribs.

No more waiting. No more guessing. No more pretending I'm not terrified and excited and completely out of my depth. Whatever comes next... it's walking through that door.

CHAPTER THIRTY
MISTY

WE WATCH A STRANGE MAN ENTER THE ROOM, AND IT takes me all of two seconds to realise he is not the doctor I saw last time. Gone is the calm, soft-spoken specialist who told me I was infertile. This man... this man looks like he stepped out of a paranormal detective novel.

His eyebrows are the first thing I notice — bushy, multicoloured, and moving up and down with every word he speaks, like they're having their own conversation. His eyes are worse. Dark brown, too sharp, too knowing. He looks at you like he's peeling back layers you didn't even know you had.

My boot taps against the plastic-coated leg of the chair, a nervous little rhythm I can't stop. Left, right, left. My stomach twists. My mind races. Run? Stay? Pretend I'm fine?

A warm, firm grip lands on my thigh. Braven. His hand radiates heat through the denim, grounding me instantly. My foot stops tapping. My breath steadies. He doesn't say a word, but the message is clear: I'm here.

Beside me, Braven is practically glowing. Enthusiasm. Pride. Awe. All of it pouring off him as the specialist talks about the baby — our baby. He's soaking up every detail like he's afraid to miss a single syllable.

I try to keep my focus, to look brave, to pretend I'm not overwhelmed by the avalanche of information being thrown at me. Foods I should eat. Vitamins I need. What to expect in each trimester. Things to avoid. Things to monitor. Things to prepare for.

Then he drops the bomb. I should refrain from shifting for another two days. After that, I can shift freely for the next four months. Keep my muscles supple. Keep my body strong.

Shift.

I can shift.

My heart stutters. My mind blanks. The only problem? I have absolutely no idea how to shift. Minor detail, apparently.

Information overload hits me like a freight train. Thank goodness LJ is scribbling notes like a woman possessed, because I'm pretty sure half of this is leaking straight out of my ears.

Before we leave, Braven and LJ make sure the next three appointments are booked, and the ultrasound is saved onto a memory stick. Blob's first official photo, well first one in front of Braven and LJ. My chest tightens at the thought.

We step out into the corridor, heading toward the car park, when LJ leans in close.

"Guys, move a little faster," she whispers. "I sense rogue wolf and cat shifters nearby. If we don't hurry, we might be in trouble."

My heart rate spikes. I glance at Braven.

His voice brushes my mind, calm but firm. *'Baby, stay calm. Don't look around. Act normal. Whoever they are, they won't attack if we don't draw attention.'*

I swallow hard and turn just enough to catch LJ's eye as I open the car door. She smiles like everything is perfectly fine.

"Come on, guys. Time for lunch and a well-earned coffee."

Ah. Right. A performance. Feed the wrong information to the shifters lurking nearby. Send them in the wrong direction. Clever witch.

I slide into the front passenger seat, buckle up, and casually hit the lock button with my elbow. LJ and Braven do the same in perfect sync. The engine rumbles to life, and the car rolls out of the parking spot.

I keep my eyes sharp, scanning for anyone approaching. Anyone watching. Anyone too still.

LJ doesn't waste time. She plants her foot down, and the car shoots forward, weaving out of the car park, down a side street, then another, then another, until we're heading toward the freeway.

"Um, LJ," I say, gripping the door handle as she takes a corner a little too enthusiastically. "Where are we going?"

She flashes me a smile. "We're taking a little trip. I think it's wise to visit my parents and see if my aunt left anything like her spell book behind at the old family home."

I stare at her. *Ha. What are you talking about?* Doesn't even begin to cover it.

CHAPTER THIRTY-ONE
MISTY

"LJ, WE'VE BEEN TRAVELLING FOR THE PAST HOUR AND a half. Where are we going exactly?" I ask, forehead leaning against the cool window. Country scenery blurs past — rolling hills to the left, flashes of water to the right. Every few minutes, another glimpse of blue catches my eye. A bay, maybe. Westernport Bay? It looks big enough.

A sign flashes by: Phillip Island — 20km.

Hmm. I doubt we're going to the island. LJ mentioned once her family lived near it, tucked up in the hills somewhere. My stomach gives a little flip — not nerves, just the car weaving through endless bends.

"We're nearly there, Misty," LJ says, smiling like she hasn't just dragged us halfway across the state. "Just making sure we're not being followed anymore."

What?

My head snaps toward her. "We were followed?"

"Misty, chill, girl." LJ waves a hand like this is normal

Tuesday behaviour. "We had a couple of cars tailing us back in the city and through the suburbs. I lost them. But I'm being extra careful, just in case."

I give her the what in the actual world look.

She sighs. "Fine. If you're that worried, we'll turn up here on the left and take the back roads."

Back roads? What back roads? I look ahead at the intersection. A sign reads The Gurdies – St Helier Road. Never heard of it. Great. We're officially in the middle of nowhere. The car turns. More trees. More bends. More narrow roads that look like they haven't seen civilisation since the 1800s. After twenty-five minutes of this, nausea hits me like a freight train.

LJ finally slows down, indicator clicking. My stomach sighs in relief. We turn into a long driveway, and before I can blink, the gate swings open on its own.

Magic. Of course.

"We've arrived," LJ says brightly. Then her face shifts, serious. "Remember, this is my family estate."

She tilts her head, listening to something I can't hear. I strain my ears — nothing. Just wind through trees.

"You'll feel the magic soon," she continues. "Maybe see a shifter or two. Don't freak out. Don't hurt anyone. We're safe here. Once we cross the threshold, no one can track our scent."

Oh. That's... actually amazing. The driveway winds through thick trees. I spot cows behind fences. Real cows. Real farm animals. How do they keep them here with shifters around? Wouldn't the animals bolt? Or sense danger? Or... I don't know. I guess I'll find out.

We pull up in front of a massive two-story ranch-style house with a wraparound verandah. It looks like something out of a country magazine — grand, warm, lived-in.

Within minutes, LJ's parents, two tall, handsome brothers, and a gorgeous little sister appear beside the car. All smiles. All warmth.

Overwhelming.

A sharp sting of jealousy hits me — quick, unexpected — followed immediately by guilt. I'm happy for her. Truly. She has a family. A real one. Loving. Present. Alive.

My eyes burn. I turn away, pretending to study the tree line until I can breathe again.

This morning, all I expected was a doctor's appointment and a quiet afternoon. Now I'm standing on a magical estate in the middle of nowhere, surrounded by shifters I didn't know existed, hoping I'm not the one who brings danger to their doorstep.

Braven's arms wrap around me from behind, warm and solid. I lean into him, drawing strength from the contact. My gaze drifts back to LJ's family — friendly faces, curious eyes.

Then— A voice slips into my mind. Female. Italian. Soft but commanding.

'Misty, it is okay. Come.'

I jerk slightly. Out loud, LJ's mum says, "Come inside. I think you will feel better after a cup of tea and maybe a lie down. It has been a busy day for you. Yes…" Her voice matches the one in my head.

I manage a nervous smile and nod. "Si, Mrs Bianchi."

She beams. "Come sì." Then, with a wave toward the house, "Andiamo."

Right. *Let's go.*

Braven leans close, breath warm against my ear. "Ah, baby... what did she just say?"

I turn slightly. "Let's go."

"Huh."

I tug his hand and repeat, slower, "She said, let's go."

"Ahhh."

And with that, we step toward the house — into LJ's world, into magic, into whatever comes next.

CHAPTER THIRTY-TWO
BRAVEN

WHAT AM I DOING HERE? Keeps floating around my mind, while looking around the darkened room, from the double bed Misty and I have been allocated for four nights now here at the homestead of Mr and Mrs Bianchi. With Misty snuggled tightly to my side, and her head on my chest and my arms wrapped tightly around her body?

With a strong presence of magic in the air, my phone is not fully functioning. I had soon realised shortly after arriving at this property, it must have wards surrounding it, thus preventing my mobile phone from making any outside calls, including the internet. All I can say is, how am I meant to know where I am?

I have no understanding of where I am and who has been following us. Especially when Mr Bianchi explained, we are not to leave for a couple more days at least — I'm feeling not just lost, but unworthy. What kind of mate are I, when I am apparently failing to protect Misty and our unborn baby? What kind of man am I if I am not able to protect the ones I love?

While drinking coffee after breakfast the morning after we arrived, Mr Bianchi and several other relations of LJ's, informed me we are located near the small town situated along the Bass Highway.

They went on and explained a little about the town's history — a town named after the man himself who travelled up the local river in an open whaleboat with a crew of six, back in 1797, George Bass. They must have been nuts or extremely brave to travel around in a little boat like that.

Over the last couple of days, I have been asking questions, many questions. Why do I have the feeling I am missing something very important, especially when I noticed our hosts avoided some of my questions regarding my parents. Tomorrow things will change. I require answers, and somehow, we have to figure out how to reveal Misty's cat.

This is one topic the women elders seem to avoid discussing in front of me. I don't know what is going on around here, but my mate needs to learn how to fight and shift as quickly as possible, because if my family catches up to us, Misty is going to be in for the fight of her life.

"Braven, what's wrong? You should be asleep," Misty quietly murmurs.

I turn my head enough to see the outline of Misty's face hiding in the shadows of the room.

"Hey, baby. You should be sleeping. You need the rest."

"Braven, do not start with me," Misty replies. I can sense you are worried and stressed. Why?" She gives me a determined look with a raised brow. "We are safe here. No one can find us. So please relax. You, too, need your sleep."

I lean forward, press my lips to her warm head, and tighten my arm around her. "I love you, my mate. Now, it's time for sleep, you need your rest."

Misty replies in a soft, sleepy murmur, "Okay."

Misty's breathing has slowed back to her deep breaths within a few minutes. If only I could fall asleep that quickly.

I REACH BESIDE ME FOR MISTY, ONLY TO FIND THE BED cold and empty. With a massive morning wood eager to be put to use, I would have preferred my mate here instead of waking up alone.

I wonder what time it is, for the bright sunshine to be shining through the thin gap in the curtains the way it is, it has to be later than I think it is. I reach out with our mate link to Misty. Only to come up empty. I feel unsettled and soon realise — Misty is not in the bathroom or anywhere near me. Where is she?

I quickly got up and dressed as fast as I could. I hope Misty is with the others somewhere in this big house. Surely, she is safe here amongst the witches and shifters. I soon made quick work of my morning routine in the bathroom before attempting to track down my mate.

I make my way down the hallway; the aroma of coffee permeates the air, filling my nostrils. My belly starts to grumble with hunger and the need for caffeine. I scan the brightly lit kitchen and notice that Misty is not here. Okay, where is my mate? I take a deep breath and try to calm my cat and myself before I do something I might later regret. I release my breath before taking another deep breath in. Picking up a faint trace of Misty, her essence is a few hours old. Where is she?

With a cheerful face, Mrs Bianchi slowly approaches me with a toothy smile.

"Mr O'Geary, you are wondering where your mate is, Si?"

With a nod of my head, I continue to glance around. LJ and her aunt are not here either. I wonder if they are together. Hmm. Maybe, they might be discussing Misty's parents. I hope so, because if Misty is not here somewhere with them...my cat is going to go crazy until I find her.

"Mr O'Geary, please sit. Have a cup of coffee and some food. You should be hungry; do you know what time it is?"

I pause and wonder what Mrs Bianchi is getting at. What does she mean? Do I know what time it is?

I slide my mobile phone out of my pocket and turn it on to read the time.

Holy shit. Where did the day go? How in the world have I managed to sleep until 2.00 p.m.? Sleeping and not knowing or sensing my mate is not by my side, what has happened to me?

I glance back up into Mrs Bianchi's caring, aged eyes. I know how to be patient. This might be an old woman in front of me, but she is also crafty and intimidating, with magical power.

With a nod of her head and a teasing smile, Mrs Bianchi gives me the impression she has somehow just read my mind.

"Si, Braven. I can pick up certain thoughts, some but not all. Besides, at this very minute, your face is giving you away...

you are worried for your mate. As you should be. Plus, you cannot work out how you have slept for so long, Si."

A frown forms on my face, my eyes squint towards the little woman in front of me. I do not know to be worried or not regarding someone other than my mate being able to pick up my thoughts.

"Mrs Bianchi, yes, I am concerned about the safety of my mate. I should be beside her to protect her, not sleeping in an empty bed."

With a little laugh and a pat of her weathered hand against my arm, Mrs Bianchi replies, "Oh, Braven. You needed the sleep, young man. How are you going to protect Misty when you are exhausted?" With a lift of her chin, and a glint in her eye, why do I have the feeling I am missing something here? "Anyway, Misty is safe and needed some time to speak privately with my sister. And my sister refused to discuss anything in front of you."

Ha. Why? What did I do?

"What my sister has to discuss with young Misty is for her ears, only. When Misty feels the time is right, she will inform you what has been discussed today. Though I would not be holding my breath, chances are, my sister will tell her not to tell you anything."

Whoa. What...why? I feel confused about Mrs Bianchi's words. I slowly sit down at the kitchen table. Before I realise it, I have a steaming cup of coffee in my hand and a plate of piping hot food in front of me.

I can feel my belly grumble once more and slowly lift the fork to feed myself, one mouthful at a time.

Chapter Thirty-Three
Misty

"Come on, Misty, concentrate. You just about did it before...you can do it," LJ's voice breaks my concentration. Grrrr

Even though I am feeling annoyed and extremely frustrated, I try to focus. If LJ speaks one more time, I am going to pounce on her.

I look towards my soon to be ex-friend, with her smiling, cheerful face, my hand twitches to wipe that look off her face.

How long have we been practising anyway? Surely, we can take a break. I feel another drip of sweat roll down my face and back. I reckon I need to take a break.

"Ms Misty, concentrate. We have removed the blocking spell; you should start to feel the presence of your animal inside you. Now, come... Concentrate on your cat. Feel your cat. Speak to your cat. Your cat is part of you. Become one with your animal."

Uh-huh. I will just speak with my cat shall I, as my cat is

part of me? I do not know if I can really do this. But I will try once again.

With the previous lessons running through my head, I concentrate again on my inner body, rehashing and going over the step-by-step instructions. After a few seconds or minutes, not sure which, I pause to a strange sensation. I start to feel and sense something within my mind. I do not know if it is shock or disbelief as something moves within my mind's eye. A dark shape forms, becoming larger until it begins to form the shape of an animal — my cat!

Holy shit...

The more I focus, the more she becomes clear. Oh, my goodness... Shocked and overwhelmed, I continue to stare into my mind, watching this magnificent animal.

She is a beautiful, feisty one. But then, that's understandable considering she has been locked away all these years. At least she is not angry with me, just the witches who locked her away.

I feel her growl towards the mention of witches, and I don't blame her. When I was listening to LJ's aunt explain in great detail, we have both come to the same conclusion, the blocking of my shifting was for our safety. Even though we do not agree with what happened, it was best to protect the pair of us.

That is something which is still confusing me. Why did I need such protection? This is the annoying part of my question which has not been fully revealed to me.

With everything I have learnt and practised today, my brain is having an overload episode. Feeling Braven trying to reach out to me, searching for me, I can feel how worried and concerned he is for me. It is incredible to learn the skills to feel, block, and search for my mate. Things I would have discovered if I had been raised amongst the shifters.

LJ's aunt — Mrs Gratino, or Shirley. Yeah, the name Shirley just does not resemble the woman in front of me. However, Shirley explained, for now, I have to block Braven and concentrate on my cat. I give — her — my gorgeous cat, my attention — and love. I have to learn to speak to her — feel her — and touch her. I have to prepare myself for the change, prepare to shift into my cat form, and remember to turn back to my human body — no pressure.

Shirley has pushed the issue. Now I have been learning the basics of my hidden heritage. I will be able to master specific abilities. Abilities I never knew I had. It turns out I also have a small amount of magic running through my veins.

With Shirley's help, I will be able to tap into it finally, and begin to feel the strange sensations of magic in the air, caressing my skin like a delicate silk scarf.

I mentally connect once again with my feisty cat, concentrating as hard as I can. A quiet voice starts to emerge amongst the barrage of images and feelings — a voice building in strength and volume.

'Malisty concentrate harder, that is it, you are finally doing it. Come on. We are nearly there. Remember, I will protect our precious babies.'

With those words rushing through my mind, I suddenly open my eyes.

What in the world...glancing all around, trying to see who is speaking to me, for me only to see LJ and her aunt – Shirley.

Who was that? And, what did they mean, babies? I am not carrying babies; I am only carrying one baby. A strange sensation travels through my head as if someone is somehow caressing my mind from within, followed by the voice I heard before, speaking once more.

'*Malisty concentrate, and we will shift.*'

Whoa. What in the world is happening? Who is speaking to me?

'*Malisty, don't be silly,*' the voice says in a gruff female tone in my head. '*For the first time in all these years, we are starting to communicate with one another again.*'

Huh... Communicate...again? I concentrate on the voice and mentally reach towards it and say.

'*What do you mean by communicate again? Who and where are you?*'

'*Oh, Malisty. You really do not remember, do you?*'

Remember what?

With a sigh, the voice replies, '*Me. Malisty, me.*'

Still not seeing anyone else around us, I ask, '*Who are you?*'

'I am you. You are me. We are one — together. I am your animal half.'

Whoa, a minute and back up.

I take in a harried breath as I quickly glance around. It does not take me long to notice LJ giving me strange looks. I then glance towards her aunt and see a big smile forming on her face before her lips start to move before speaking.

"Misty, I think you have finally achieved your connection with your cat...yes?"

With a small nod of my head, I do not know what to believe now. Since when do people speak with imaginary voices in their head?

I hear a small chuckle, before the voice replies, *'Since you became a shifter, Malisty. Once upon a time, you and I always spoke with one another. Until that bad witch and our parents hid me from your mind and memories, preventing me from appearing when you hit puberty.'*

Oh no.

Then it is all true. My parents really did prevent me from shifting and hid my cat from me, magically.

'Yes, Malisty. That is the case. I can understand why. Nevertheless, it still hurts, to have been shunned the way I have. It was, after all, for our protection. Soon you will meet our other little friend.'

Huh, what is the voice speaking about? What other — little friend?

'Excuse me, but what do I call you? And, what is this other little friend you speak of?'

'Oh, Malisty. There has been so much hidden and kept from you. In time, you will learn all. However, for now, the meeting with our other little friend will have to be kept secret for now. I'll say, for now, so you will not panic on me. The animal form you'll shift into depends on the soulmate you conceived with.'

'Huh? What does that have to do with it all?'

'Malisty, when you are pregnant, you can only change forms into the animal you have mated with...'

'What are you talking about? I just have one mate.'

'No, Malisty. You have two soulmates. One cat shifter and the other is a wolf shifter.'

'No, there must be some mistake? I have only mated with Braven.'

'No, Malisty. There is no mistake. You are extremely special and unique.'

'What do you mean special and unique?'

'What I am failing to explain is — when your belly is not carrying a cub — you will be able to shift into either animal. That is the reason why your parents fled with you, and hid because your ability to shape-shift into either a cat or a wolf.'

'I don't understand, how can that—'

'Your life became a death sentence the moment it had been discovered you would be able to shift into either a wolf or large cat, once puberty started.'

'No. There must be some mistake...'

I continue to shake my head. I don't know to be in denial or not. My emotions and feelings are that tense; it feels they are ready to snap at any second. Even though all this shifter stuff is new to me, somehow, I can detect and sense the truth coming from my inner animal, this voice inside my mind.

'There is something else you need to be made aware of.'

Oh, terrific, what else is there? What else is there to be made aware of? Somehow, I need to pull up my big girl panties and ask what else there is to know — here goes...

'What else is there to discover, then — I am a shifter of two different animals, and my life is in danger.'

'Malisty we bumped into your other soulmate — your wolf mate in that supermarket recently.'

I begin to think back to the day I arrived in Lakes Entrance, I hope the female voice in my head is not speaking about one of those homeless guys, but the...

'What... You don't mean that delicious smelling, that scrumptious looking guy at the DVDs? The guy I had those weird feelings for... The same guy who I had been sure I knew that we had met somewhere previously.'

'Yes,' Is all the voice said.

'But how? He is married. Who is he?'

'That male wolf is Xavier. He married someone else because he thought you to be dead. After all both he and your cat shifter mate – Braven, had both been told you had been killed in a car accident. Xavier married his teenage girlfriend. If you had stayed near him longer, he would have recognised you as a wolf shifter.'

'But hang on, how can that be? Braven has only sensed me as a cat shifter...how can that be?'

'Remember how I said you are extremely unique? Until the day you are able to shift into either your animal forms, Braven will only sense the cat in you. And your wolf mate will only detect your wolf. Until we know whom we can trust, we have to keep this information secret; otherwise, your life will be forfeit if the wrong people know you will be able to shift into either a cat or wolf.'

'Okay... keep my shifting ability secret, or die.' Now for a change of topic. *'You said, babies, ...how can that be. The scan only suggested one foetus.'*

The tone of her voice changed with a smugness, which quickly became annoying.

'Well, now. As your mate is exceptionally virile, he has managed to impregnate you again.'

'Huh.'

With her tone changing to severe, the voice said, *'Malisty, please listen. Until Braven can stop his body, his cat will continue the mating process until it is satisfied with the pregnancy, and your belly is full of his cubs.'*

Oh, shit...

'You can say that again.'

I listen to Marni. Yes, Marni, the name of the voice in my head, who just happens to be in charge of my shifter animals. She had been aware of everything happening to me all through the years...only she had no say or influence in my life. Her destiny was to remain silent...she had been held captive within my mind, until now.

If only I had known about her and my secret, hidden past.

Usually, with shifters, they do not have a separate voice floating in their head, as I do. Most shifters feel their animal, and their voice as combined, as one giving the impression the human is one with their animal — one being. I happen to be different. What else is new!

I FOLLOW MARNI'S INSTRUCTIONS, AND IT DOES NOT take me long to accomplish the ability to shift fluently into my big, sleek black beautiful cat for the first time.

As if they belong to a newborn, I feel my legs shake and tremble beneath me — all four of them! Wow. I still cannot believe the vision in front of my eyes as I looked down between my front, sleek furry legs and towards the sight of my new back legs with wicked looking cat clawed feet, or should I say paws.

But then...

I continue to blink several times, and try to focus on my surroundings, noticing the depth of colour and small particles in the air. Wow, my eyesight is better now than when I am in my human form. Lifting my head, I soon notice the weight difference — my head feels heavy. It looks like I will be starting some serious exercise to strengthen my muscles, especially those in my neck.

Oh, my goodness, that rocking sensation coming from behind me feels strange. With a sway of my hips, I turn my head and see a long narrow furry tail swishing from side to side, causing my back legs to stagger.

What the?

No really?

I have a tail...

Holy shit. I have a tail.

My breathing increases along with my heart rate, beating faster with each breath I take. I think I might be having either a heart attack or an anxiety attack.

Oh boy. Is this happening? Bugger my parents for hiding my shifter side from me. If I had been aware of my heritage, I would know how to shift, walk, and be one with my cat.

I scan over my sleek body, and my new strange tongue runs over my sharp teeth. Oh, wow. Sharp teeth. Holy cow. Slowly opening my mouth, I search my mouth a little more, noticing just how long my newly shaped tongue really is.

My new body is going to take some getting used to. Me, a cat shifter!

Still, in my cat form, my thoughts soon fill my mind. *Baby. Oh no, the baby.* With my mind, I quickly contact the voice in my head — Marni.

'Marni, how is the baby? My shift did not harm the baby, did it?'

After a second or two, Marni finally replies, *'Malisty, I can sense all three foetuses are unharmed.'*

Say what... three foetuses. Triplets? Holy shit. Noooo...

CHAPTER THIRTY-FOUR
MISTY

TWO HOURS LATER, FEELING FATIGUED AND HUNGRY, I decide it is time to head back to the house and eat some food, shower, find my mate and sleep. Looking towards LJ and Shirley, I hope they will agree with me. Marni has already advised me that I will not handle another shift without rest and food first.

I sense Braven approaching from behind, his concern and worry surrounding my senses. Uh-oh, he can feel how hungry and tired I am. I wonder if he has something to eat with him? By the time I turned around, looked up, and scanned my surroundings, my handsome mate approached me, with a smile on his face and annoyance in his eyes.

I watch his eyes squint towards LJ and narrow, especially when he stares at Shirley, I see his white-knuckled hands fisted and slowly open by his side, keeping his anger under control.

"Good afternoon, ladies. How is everything progressing?" He says through clenched teeth. Oh, my. Braven seems a bit pissed off. I wonder what is going on? Does it have anything to do with me?

Braven turns his head towards me and tries to smile but fails.

"Misty. Baby. I think it might be time for rest and eat. You have been out here all day."

With a small nod of my head, I agree with him. I step towards Braven as I say to Shirley, "Thank you, Shirley, for your instructions. I will make sure to keep practising."

I place a smile on my face and look towards the woman who has been encouraging and teaching me these past few days, when I reach Braven's side that is when I notice the strange glint in her eyes. What is with the look? Before I can blink, her strange look is replaced with her friendly smiling face.

"Misty, make sure to keep practising, young lady. The more you practice, the quicker and easier it will be to shift to your cat."

LJ approaches my side and whispers, "Girl, go eat and rest. We'll catch up later."

Between his clenched teeth, Braven replies, "No, LJ. I can feel that Misty requires rest. She has overdone it. No more lessons for her today."

CHAPTER THIRTY-FIVE
BRAVEN

I CAN FEEL HOW DRAINED AND EXHAUSTED MISTY had become. I hold her in my arms while she slept. Relief — knowing Misty is away from the witches and finally resting, means I can keep an eye on her while protecting her. Bloody witches.

The impression I have of these local witches — they are hiding something. There is more to what happened to Misty all those years ago than what the witches have so far revealed.

I feel my anger raging within, and I try to keep it under control, so I don't wake Misty.

One thing I have noticed since I caught up with Misty this afternoon, I can feel her cat. Not just sensing she is a cat shifter, but her actual cat. Hmmm. Usually, you do not detect someone's cat as an individual entity like this.

The only thing I am not able to place my finger on is that there is something slightly different regarding Misty and her shifting ability — with her cat. When Misty wakes later, I will speak with my mate and watch her shift. I need to see and touch her cat for myself. Something is different, and I do not know what it is, but I am determined to find out.

FROM THE DEPTHS OF MY SLUMBER, A VOICE CALLED to me, screaming for me to wake up and listen...

Who in the world is waking me up?

Just leave me alone to sleep, and be wrapped around my mate.'

Oh shit, my mate.

Within seconds, reality hits. I can feel a warm body struggling beside me, thrashing about.

Before my tired brain can register anything, a limb, no a hand strikes out, connecting with my face.

Whack. Hard enough to hurt, nearly causing it to bleed.

Ah, fuck. What is going on?

With one hand, I gingerly touch my sensitive nose. I move slightly and quickly scan the room for any threats, finding none. I look back down at my restless mate. Just narrowly dodging another fist to the face. It does not take me long to realise that Misty is in the process of a bad dream.

'Not a dream.'

I hear a faint voice inside my head, and I glance

around the room once again, searching, listening, determining where the sound is coming from, and not seeing anyone.

Since when can anyone breach my mind shields? This has me stumped.

'Braven, wake up. You need to wake Malisty. You might think she is dreaming; she is not. Our girl at this very moment is being assaulted...from within her mind.'

What the hell. Assault. What...?

With my mind, I demand, *'Who are you? How are you in my mind? And what do you mean, Malisty is being assaulted? Misty is fast asleep, right here.'*

'Braven, it has been a very long time since we have spoken. However, this small talk is not addressing the problem. Malisty's mind is under siege. Now I need you as her soulmate to wake her up. Now.'

'Okay. Okay. As soon as we can, whoever you are, we are going to talk. Right now, my mate comes first.'

I stare down at Misty and look at her face. I can see she is in pain and upset. I have also noticed that I am not able to reach into Misty's mind, and this has me worried.

Carefully reaching out, I gently touch and stroke Misty's warm flesh. My voice is quiet and soft as I attempt to reassure Misty that I am here for her.

"Misty, baby. Wake up. You're having a bad dream. Wake up, Misty."

I repeat myself several times until I can see Misty start to acknowledge my voice.

In a frantic voice, Misty murmurs, "Braven. Where are you? Help me."

Ahh, shit.

What in the world is happening to her?

"Misty, baby. I'm here. I am right here, baby. It is time to come back to me."

A little louder in my alpha voice, I command, "Come back to me now, Misty."

I feel Misty pause, and the dominant alpha side of my cat is pushing for me to speak again. At least my alpha tone can break through to her mind.

"Come back to me now, Misty," I growl and watch as her eyes flutter open, before taking a deep breath.

Her eyes start to focus before they turn towards me. With a frown on her gorgeous face, Misty asks, "Braven? What is going on? Why are you waking me?"

Oh, thank fuck. Misty is waking.

"Hello, baby. You had a bad dream."

With another frown, I can see Misty struggling to remember what had just occurred.

With a small shake of her head, she whispers, "Really. I d... don...don't remember. Did I say anything out loud?"

I attempt to slip back into Misty's mind and finally succeed. Apart from her mind being foggy with sleep, I can sense another presence, well, a couple actually, and I do not like it one bit. Who in the hell has been in her mind?"

Chapter Thirty-Six
Misty

WHAT IN THE WORLD IS GOING ON?

The more I wake, the more I can feel, no, sense something is wrong.

With my mind, I reach out to connect with my other half, Marni.

'Marni are you there? What is going on? And why do I feel as if something is not right?'

Within seconds, I feel the presence of Marni, and finally, her voice fills my head, *'It is good to have you back, Malisty. I will be honest with you. It was not a dream you had been having.'*

'What do you mean I was not dreaming? What was happening, then?'

'Malisty, you are no longer safe here. Someone has discovered you are here. We must leave before they come.'

'What do you mean I am not safe here? I am in a house full of witches and shifters. I think I am protected enough.'

'Malisty, get your arse out of bed and get dressed. Tell your mate to move it also. I think it is time to wake LJ up. She can drive.'

'Marni, what is really happening?'

'Malisty, please get out of bed and move. We do not have long before they arrive.'

'Who? Who is arriving?'

'Please, Malisty; get out of the bed. NOW.' Marni demands.

'Okay, I'll move, but you better keep talking, sister.'

'I'll fill you in, but please hurry. All our lives are at stake.'

As I quickly untangle myself from the warmth of Braven, I look towards him and say, "Braven, we are in danger. We have to leave now. Someone is coming, and we must leave before it is too late."

With a wary glance, Braven says, "Who is coming, Misty?"

I stand up to find my legs are shaky beneath me. I lock my knees to prevent my legs from collapsing and reply, "Marni my cat is warning us. I have been discovered, and we have to leave immediately. Before it is too late."

I watch Braven from the corner of my eye as I quickly throw on some clothes. Braven does the same and promptly dresses. Pulling on my socks and a pair of shoes, I grab my bag and phone and dial LJ's number.

I listen to it ring through the speaker, and she answers on the fourth ring. Next, I hear LJ's groggy voice, "What is going on, Misty? Why are you awake..." LJ pauses. She must be looking at the clock. "Oh shit, Misty, do you know what the time is?"

With urgency bombarding my senses, I feel Marni push me to move faster. I reach for the bedroom door handle and answer, "LJ, I am in danger, and that danger is about to come to your doorstep. We have to leave right now before it is too late. I'll meet you at your car. Please hurry."

LJ starts to speak, and I end the call before she can say another word.

Braven starts to speak from behind me, "Misty, you said your cat, Marni, said you are in danger, and we have to leave. What else is Marni telling you?"

With a worried look, I say, "We must leave now. Come on. I'll meet you outside."

I take off as quietly as possible and head for the nearest exit. Once I open the door, the chill from the late night caresses my face, and I shiver from the cold. Glad I had thrown my jumper on now, as I began to run towards LJ's car.

Within a minute, Braven is behind me, and LJ is racing towards us in a panic.

With her keys in her hand, she hits the key fob to release the door locks, and all three of us quickly open a car door each and slide in. It is not long before LJ has the engine started, the car in drive, and her foot on the accelerator.

Constantly looking around us, I wonder how close the danger is.

'Marni, do you know how close the danger is?'

'Yes, they are nearly here, they will be advancing at the front entrance. Instruct LJ to go to the back entrance of the property. Quickly, Malisty.'

I glance towards LJ and say, "LJ, we need to head to the property's back entrance. The danger is approaching from the front. Quickly, please, LJ."

With a shocked look and a nod of her chin, LJ quickly turns the steering wheel and heads the car in another direction. I watch the trees fly by, and the heads of the animals rapidly turn and watch us as the car speeds along the dirt track.

I glance at the rear-vision mirror and see the house lights in the distance start to turn on.

"LJ, did you warn the others of the approaching danger?"

"Yes, Misty. As I was leaving, I started the warning system. I knew you were telling me the truth. Some of our protection wards had been breached. So I knew to take your warning to heart."

Relief fills me, knowing the others have been warned.

With an annoyed tone, LJ asks, "Now, are you going to tell me what is going on, and how you knew danger was approaching the property?"

I look back through the windscreen, and I can see a closed gate in front of us. As we approach, the gate starts to open. Oh, thank goodness for that.

We race through the open gateway and onto the road. I am glad LJ knows her way around these back roads.

"LJ, I really do not know much, my cat warned me. We were in danger, and we had to leave."

"Your cat... Really, Misty? You're tellin' me, your cat spoke to you and warned you of the impending danger. Is that about right...?"

"Yes, LJ. That is right. My cat speaks to me. She said we used to speak to one another like this when I was still a little girl before your aunt placed Marni in status."

"Marni..."

"Yes. Marni. That is my cat. Marni is her name."

"Oh, girl. We have some serious talking to do. But right now, I have to concentrate on gettin' us out of here — at the same time, for us not to be followed."

I watch LJ drive like a professional racecar driver around the twists and turns of the back roads. She has kept the headlights of the car off, most likely to prevent anyone from seeing us leave. Thankfully, LJ seems to have fantastic night vision at this time of night, and no other vehicles have appeared. As soon as we return to the main road, LJ turns the car headlights on and plants her foot down. With the occasional random car approaching and thankfully no car headlights behind us, we race towards Melbourne.

Chapter Thirty-Seven
Misty

We finally step into LJ's apartment, it is not long before my belly starts grumbling, and Braven's face becomes concerned.

The sound of a female voice clearing her throat, in my head alerts me Marni has something to say.

'Malisty, you need to eat and drink.'

'Thanks for the update, Marni. With my belly grumbling, I already came to that conclusion. By the way, how are the babies?'

'Don't be spiteful. And... Yes. All the foetuses are thriving and growing.'

'Marni, are you able to detect if we are safe here?'

'I have been monitoring us since we left the farm. As long as LJ sets the wards and removes our scent, we should be okay. As for you, Malisty, you need to eat.'

'Okay. Okay, Marni. I will grab something to eat as soon as the apartment is safe.'

I glance up towards LJ, and I think it is time to remind her to set her wards and cover our scent before any other shifters try to make an appearance.

"COME ON, BRAVEN. WE HAVE BEEN HERE FOR TWO weeks. I need to go to the office."

I have had it — I feel anxious and stir-crazy. I don't know how much more I can handle being cooped up in LJ's apartment. With all the practice I have been doing, I think I have mastered shifting into my cat form, within a three-second time frame. I had been worried about Braven seeing my shift, but as it turns out, he is so proud of me, especially witnessing me shift so quickly.

At least I know, Braven's cat also loves my cat and me. Marni said that when she had detected Braven's cat when we were children; she had fallen in love with him too.

I move towards the windows and carefully glance out, admiring the city view. While I have been cooped up here, I have kept in contact with my contractors. All the renovations to my new apartment are coming along. The contractor informed me, they are ahead of schedule, which is a relief. Paying my bills and chatting with my contractor online has helped me from going completely insane.

LJ's hidden safe room has come in handy for my shifting practising, and with LJ's help, I have also mastered the art of fighting. It is a relief to know if I ever need to fight and protect myself, I can. All those lessons I had as a teenager are finally paying off. LJ is extremely proud of my progress.

Braven had not been keen on the idea of me shifting and learning new skills, but deep down, I think he knows these new skills will be required for that one day when he is not around to protect me. That is just the thing; he will never be able to protect me 24/7.

As far as Braven is concerned, he will always be by my side to protect our babies and me. Yes, he became very smug when he detected the new foetuses. Hopefully, his cat will be happy and stop trying to impregnate me again. Now I have to work out, for some time, and for alone time. He is starting to smother me.

Chapter Thirty-Eight
Braven

WHAT THE HELL AM I GOING TO DO?

I have my mother texting me, informing me I am needed back at our clan land. My father is meant to be sick, and I need to take my rightful place at the head of the clan. To look after our pack, before my brother tries to bulldoze his way in and destroy everything my family has built over the last six decades.

Should I trust my mother? Yet, my gut is telling me, everything she has said is lies.

I hear another ding, alerting me my phone has just received another text. I look down at the screen, and I can see my mother has sent another message.

MOTHER:

Braven, please come home. I do not know what to do. Your father is getting worse, and I do not know how much longer he has.

Stupidly, I text back.

ME:

Mum. I am not able to leave right now. The elders know what to do. Speak to them.

MOTHER:

The elders have turned their backs on us.

ME:

Mother, the elders, would never turn their backs on us. Our family has always been alpha of the clan. They need us.

MOTHER:

Braven, I don't know what your father has done, but the money is gone.

What the fuck... There has to be some type of mistake.

ME:

Mother, what is really going on? I am busy with my mate. The mate, my father, wanted to hurt. I am not going to come rushing back and leave my mate unprotected.

MOTHER:

Your mate will be safe, especially when you become alpha.

I begin to feel edgy regarding these text messages. I guess

one way to know if the person sending me these messages are from my mother or not...

ME:

> Mum, can you send me a picture of the front gardens. I want to show my mate, some of the plants.

MOTHER:

> Braven I do not have time to take pictures. Now come home. ASAP.

If the other person were my mother, she would have asked, 'What front plants?' Therefore, I now know, someone else has my mother's phone.

ME:

> Sorry, but I am not able to leave anytime soon.

MOTHER:

> You disappoint me, my son. I always thought you would be there for your family and clan.

Wow. Now that is a bit below the belt — a real low blow. And from the way the wording is, it is either my brother, Marcus or father on the other end of these messages.

Let me think. I think it might be wise to play along and give them the false sense I will leave soon. I need to know what type of games they are playing.

ME:

I have always been there for the clan. It is a pity you think that way. Once I have sorted a few other tasks out, I will be on my way home.

MOTHER:

You had better make sure to be back here soon.

If this person had been my mother, she would never have said that in a text.

I switch my phone off; I refuse to play these stupid games. I had better head down to the nearest store and purchase another phone. I cannot continue using this mobile if my phone is being tracked.

I listen out for Misty, and all I hear is her deep breathing. She has been practising far too much, with her shifting. I just hope she does not overdo it. I'll leave a note and allow her to continue sleeping. She needs the rest, especially now that I know she carries more of my cubs. My cat is incredibly proud to make sure our mate's belly is full of our cubs and in a big way, so am I.

I return to the kitchen, find a notepad and pen, and quickly jot down a message for Misty. I leave my note in the middle of the bench for Misty to see. If she wakes before I arrive back, she will know where I am. Glancing around the apartment, I know Misty will be safe here while I am gone.

I grab my wallet and phone, quietly open and close the door behind me, and silently make my way down the hallway towards the elevator and hit the down button. With the ding of the elevator door opening, I casually walk into the empty elevator and tap the ground-level button. It is not long before the doors open once again, and I step out of the elevator. Not seeing anyone, I start to head for the nearest exit.

The only warning I had was hearing someone behind me. I started to turn my head, but before I could see who it was, I was tackled hard to the ground. I feel a stinging pinch to my neck, and something dark is pulled over my face. Before I can think much about anything, I try to move my limbs, only to find that my body is not responding to me.

Oh shit, I'm in trouble.

With a heavy fog descending over my brain, I have no idea who has attacked me. I try again to move my head, it is no use, as everything starts to turn dark, and my thoughts turn to Misty.

'I love you, my mate, and I am sorry.'

CHAPTER THIRTY-NINE
MISTY

I KNEW THERE WAS SOMETHING SERIOUSLY WRONG before I fully woke up. With my senses on high alert, I reach out to my mate, only to find Braven was not in the apartment.

No one was in the apartment. I'm alone.

I push my senses further out to the surrounding apartments — nothing — no sign of Braven whatsoever.

Even LJ is not back yet. Where in the world is everyone? How did I manage to be alone in the apartment? Why am I sensing something is very wrong?

The old saying — be careful what you wish for — comes to mind. Yes, I wanted space, but something is wrong. I can feel and sense it.

I reach over to my mobile phone and quickly turn it on. I see no messages from Braven or LJ. I am a little shocked when I notice the time on the screen, how in the world have I remained asleep until early evening? Why has no one woken me before now?

I crawl out of bed and use the bathroom before getting dressed and walk into the empty kitchen.

I survey the room, finding nothing out of place, before walking up to the fridge to grab a bottle of water. As I start to drink the cold water to quench my dry throat, I notice a piece of paper sitting on the kitchen bench.

With a trembling hand, I reach over and pick the paper up. The first thing I notice is Braven's handwriting. I scan his neat, elegant scrawl, quickly reading over his written message. Braven says he is going down the street to purchase a new mobile phone. His family have been hassling him, and he does not want them to track him down by using his mobile phone.

What was Braven thinking to go out by himself...if anything has happened to him?

Oh, no...

With my mind, I quickly reach out and contact Marni.

'Marni, are you there? Can you hear me or read the note Braven has left? Have you felt something is wrong?'

Sensing Marni's presence, hearing her voice in my head, relief hits me, knowing I am not entirely alone.

'Malisty, glad to see you are awake. I hate to break it to you, but Braven is in serious trouble. I have been trying to contact his cat, but whatever happened to him — is bad, very bad. I am no longer able to reach his cat. I think he has been drugged and taken.'

What? No. No, no, no, no, no. That cannot be right.

Chapter Forty
Misty

Within two hours, with assistance from LJ's family — who can be scary when they want to be, we managed to discover Braven is on the move and heading towards Lakes Entrance. I am incredibly grateful for their support in using their extraordinary talent and skills in finding and tracking Braven.

Scary. But terrific.

With this piece of information, the only conclusion we can come up with is Braven's family is behind his abduction.

LJ and I start on our way towards Lakes Entrance, with LJ behind the wheel. We decided it would be safer for LJ to drive and allow me to rest and concentrate on reaching Braven through our mate bond.

So far, everything I have tried has failed to connect to my mate, which makes me worry more with each passing minute.

'Marni, have you been able to contact Braven's cat. Can you detect him at all?'

'No, Malisty. Something is blocking our connection. Never fear. I will continue to reach out and try to establish a connection.'

'Keep trying, Marni. Let me know as soon as you feel them. I need to know Braven is okay. I...I'm...'

'I know, Malisty, I know. Just try to keep yourself calm. You have to look after yourself and the babies.'

I feel overwhelmed, confused, annoyed, and useless sitting here in LJ's car. I need to do something. I have to...

'Malisty. Stop it, right now. You are upsetting yourself.' Marni abruptly interrupts my mind rant.

'Listen to me, young lady. You have to calm down, and you need to focus. There is a significant possibility you will be required to fight when we find Braven.'

What? Why would I need t—

'Malisty, if what I am suspecting is correct, this little arrangement with Braven mysteriously being taken is only a setup to lure you back to Lakes Entrance. Braven's father wants you.'

'Me? Why would his father want me? What have I done to attract his attention?'

'Oh, my poor girl. His father wants you because he has never had you — that is why. You belong to his son, meaning he thinks he can have you.'

'If my memories are right, I do not like Braven's father, and he is a cruel, sexist man.'

'Yes, Malisty, Braven's father can never be trusted. Always remember that. He lies, and he takes what he wants.'

'Marni, why do I have the feeling that there is another reason for my presence back at the clan and Lakes Entrance?'

'Because there most likely is, and that other reason is Braven's ex-fiancé, who I can guarantee will want to challenge you in a death fight.'

'A death fight. What are you talking about?'

With a sigh, Marni explains.

'A death fight between the shifters is a way for one shifter to kill and take the other's mate legally. Providing the wanted mate survives the death of their fallen mate, of course.'

'How barbaric. And this is allowed in today's society?'

'Yes, Malisty. It is very much allowed. I think this is another reason for Braven to make sure you both left Lakes Entrance, to protect both of you.'

I remember the day I left Lakes Entrance and what little Braven explained once he arrived in Melbourne. I can now see how worried he had been, for a whole other reason. If only he had explained everything to me.

I look towards the car clock, then out the dark window and then back to the clock. The time finally makes sense to my brain, while I have been busy thinking, contemplating, and conversing with Marni the time has flown. LJ has been driving for three hours, I think it might be time for her to have a break and I'll take over the driving.

I glance towards LJ, and I can see the concentration on her face, witnessing her mind busy at work.

"LJ, I think we had better stop at the next big town and grab something to eat and drink. If you want, I'll take over and drive."

With a smile, LJ replied, "No, I'm fine, Misty. I'll keep driving through. I will stop at Bairnsdale, fill the car with fuel, and we'll get some food."

I'm not sure what to say, so I just nod. I can see that LJ is busy in her own mind. I wonder if she might be speaking with someone.

We pull up at the gas station within twenty minutes and fill the vehicle's fuel tank. Before I can grab my bag and get out, LJ is back with two hot cups of tea and salad rolls. So much for me getting out of the car and stretching my legs.

With my hands full, I carefully sip my hot tea, relishing the flavoured brew.

Ahh. I needed that. Placing the cup in the car drink holder, I somehow unwrap my salad roll and inhale it. Before I knew it, I had eaten every crumb, and my drink cup was empty.

Geez, I must have been hungrier than I realised.

"LJ, SPEAK TO ME, I CAN SEE YOU HAVE BEEN communicating with someone, now spill. What is happening? Do you have any news regarding Braven?" I ask urgently while my heart continues to beat faster than usual.

I hope Braven is okay. Because if he were dead, I think I would have felt something by now.

'You would have felt it, the instant it happened, Malisty. The closer we are to Lakes Entrance, the more I am sensing Braven and his cat. All we have to do is find him.'

'Is that why you have been quiet?'

'Yes. I have been trying to keep focused on Braven and his cat. At times, I have sensed them and felt their pain. Other times, it feels as if a cover or shield has been put up in place.'

'Marni, you said you had felt pain. What do you mean by that?'

'Malisty, it was only brief, but the pain I felt through our connection was terrible. Someone is torturing Braven.'

What...? Gods no.

I should have expected those creatures to torture Braven. He had left, and we knew the cat clan was searching for him.

LJ's voice brings my attention back to the interior of the car. "Misty, my people located Braven. However, my news is not all good." With a nod, I encourage LJ to continue: "The local contacts know where he is being held."

"Yes, and what did your contacts say?" Already knowing my soulmate is in pain from the horrible creatures who have taken him, and I am helpless to stop them.

"Ahh. The contacts mentioned Liasa is back, and she is the one behind the abduction. The bad piece of news is, Braven's father is involved."

"Why do I have the feeling you are leaving something out?"

"Because I am."

"Okay. So spill. What else is happening?"

"Misty, you will need to brace yourself."

"LJ, get to the point. What is happening to Braven?"

"I only just discovered where Braven is and what they have been doing to him."

I can feel my blood pressure rising, and I keep reminding myself to remain calm. What are they doing to my mate?

"What do you mean, what have they been doing to him?"

With a concerned look and biting her bottom lip, LJ pauses for a moment. Thinking. I contemplate what to say next.

Whatever it is, I now know it will not be good. Bad. Very bad.

"Well... So far I have been informed, Braven is tied naked and spread-eagled to a frame, and they are torturing him..." Oh, shit. Marni was right. What a bunch of animals. Why do they have to do that? Why torture him?

LJ pauses, I can tell just by her body language that what has been happening to Braven is more than just torture. If Liasa is involved, I can imagine her raping Braven for her own personal greed.

"Don't stop there, LJ. What else has happened?"

"Misty, I can't say it. Please don't make me."

With a shake of my head, I filled in the blanks instead.

"LJ, you mentioned Liasa has my mate. This means that Liasa will use Braven to conceive the next alpha. Am I right?"

With a nod of her head, LJ murmurs, "That's correct. I am so sorry, Misty."

"Why are you sorry, LJ? We will get him out. We both know Braven is not able to impregnate any other woman apart from his mate. Me."

"Misty, how can you remain so calm?"

With a shake of my head, I know I have to keep calm, not just for the babies and myself, but also for Braven. I think it also helped to discuss all this mess with Marni, but still, it is hard to fathom all this information. If I hope to break Braven out, I need all my wits to do it.

"I have no choice, LJ. Now, where are they holding my mate?"

Chapter Forty-One

Braven

WHAT IN THE WORLD? WHY IS MY BODY NOT responding?

I go to move my hands and arms, and yet, I am not able to move any of my limbs — nothing is happening.

I remind myself to keep calm. Darkness surrounds my eyes and a hint of, rough fabric touches my nose — something is covering my face.

What the...?

Well, that explains why I cannot see anything. I begin to concentrate on reducing my breathing and slowing my heartbeat, opening my hearing as much as possible. I need to know if I can hear anything around me.

I need to know if it is safe enough to shift to my cat form; I might be able to escape. I reach out for my cat half, only to find — nothing. What in the world... Where is my cat?

Panic starts to kick in before I can focus and concentrate on moving again. It does not take me long to realise, my body is tied up, and I am in trouble.

Oh no. What about Misty?

With my senses, I reach out. It does not take me long to determine I cannot feel, hear or sense Misty nearby. At least that is one less worry I have. All I have to determine is where I am and with whom? Somehow, I have a terrible feeling that my own family is behind my predicament.

COLD WATER, AND SWEAT TRICKLE DOWN MY FACE and back just as striking pain radiates throughout my aching muscles. I manage to open my eyes long enough to realise my head is no longer covered, maybe now I will see the bastards who captured me when they approach.

AN OVERHEAD LIGHT SHINES BRIGHTLY, THE HARSH light blinding me. I blink several times, finding my vision blurry, and my mind is thick and fuzzy in pain. I swallow down a thick lump, attempting to keep the hunger and rolling nausea at bay. I hear a door slowly open behind me. Within seconds, a sickening odour penetrates my nostrils, informing me the bitch is back.

The question of the hour when I first gained consciousness was…Why is she bloody doing this? Why go to all this trouble to abduct me, torture me, and keep me tied naked spread-eagled against a standing frame? Within a day or maybe hours of being taken, I soon learnt the hard way.

The bitch has lost her mind. To top it all off, my pathetic father is assisting with whatever sick plan and reason she has for keeping me captive. From what little I have so far overheard, they are after Misty and using me to entice her here, wherever here is.

Plus, if I live long enough, Bitch-face is determined to impregnate herself, and I know for a fact that will never happen — not with me. She should continue to fuck my brother; at least then she might succeed in conceiving and leave me the fuck alone.

How am I going to warn my mate that she is in danger if she tries to rescue me? With my father involved, I know there is a different agenda — there always is. He wants Misty for some sick reason, a reason I need to discover more sooner than later.

"Oh, good. You are awake. I thought we would have to drug you again for you to get it up so you can fuck me again. At least now, you can get it up all on your own."

"Piss off, Liasa. I would never allow my dick to go anywhere near you. Just fuck off. Go find my brother; he is the only one out of the two of us, who can get you pregnant."

"Oh, my lover. Don't you know, I am still fucking your stupid, naive brother. He thinks he will be able to stay by my side and become the new alpha," she shrugs her shoulders and pouts her bottom lip, to make her point, "Yeah. Can you believe the stupidity of him? As if your father would allow him to take over."

"Why are you even bothering with my brother? When you

are sharing my father's bed. Does my silly little brother even know he is competing with his own father to remain between your thighs?"

The look on her face confirmed my suspicions, but then, the look on Dad's face when I showed him the phone pictures told me that he was not impressed seeing his other son fucking one of his whores. I never said I noticed his scent in my house and at her place.

"How did you know?"

I keep my face blank and murmur, "Liasa, it is common knowledge. It is just that the others in the clan are keeping the information to themselves because they value their lives. The elders will know when you inform everyone you have conceived that the cub is not mine, which will place the child down the long list of shifters waiting in line to become the next alpha. You stuffed up, Liasa. My father is only using you."

"No. That is not true. Your father loves me. I will be the next female alpha."

I slowly shake my head and sigh. "Liasa, listen to yourself. My father will never allow you to be his mate or the female alpha. Plus, I think you have forgotten about my mother. She would never step down for you."

With a smug face, Liasa replies, "That is where you are wrong, Braven. Your mother will not be female alpha for much longer."

The beat of my heart speeds up, and I remind myself I must remain calm in front of this manipulating bitch. "What have you done, Liasa?" I demand.

"Me. I have not done anything. Now, as for your brother, well, I cannot speak for him."

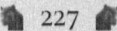

"Liasa, what the hell have you got my stupid little brother mixed into? If anything happens to my mother, my father is no longer the alpha. You do realise that, don't you?"

"No, that is not true," she whines.

"Wake up to yourself. My father is the alpha, only because of my mother. Why do you think my father has continued to keep her around, even though he fucks anything and everything else."

With uncertainty on her face, Liasa's voice trembles with worry, "No. Your father said he has a plan to get rid of her. She will no longer be part of his clan as a female alpha."

"Well, Liasa. Once my mother is no longer an alpha female, my father will lose his title. It is law, and the elders will enforce it."

Seriously, how stupid is Liasa? The rules of the local cat clan stipulated that for a male alpha to be in place, he must have an alpha female. My mother has come from an alpha family, making her an alpha female, thus allowing my father's eligibility to become the male alpha in my mother's clan.

As for myself, with my parents being alphas when I was born, I was predestined to be the next alpha. If anything happened to either of my parents, I would automatically become the next alpha. As Misty is my soulmate and not an ordinary mate, she would also become the alpha female.

Liasa is all out of luck if she believes she will become the next alpha female.

Now, all I have to work out is how in the hell I will get myself out of here and protect Misty?

Chapter Forty-Two
Misty

With a hot cup of tea between my fingers, I take another sip, letting the warmth settle in my chest while the large group of local witches and shifters crowding the dining table talk over one another. Voices clash, scrape, collide. Chairs scrape. Someone slams a palm down. Someone else hisses a disagreement. The whole room vibrates with noise and impatience.

I eye the wall clock. The minute hand ticks far too quickly, each click a punch to my ribs.

Right now, I feel wedged between a rock and a hard place, and the rock is starting to crack. We need to do something — now. I can finally sense Braven again, but the connection is faint, frayed. His fatigue bleeds into me. His pain pulses through my bones. Every second we waste is another second he suffers.

'Malisty, I have had enough of these idiots. No one has an ideal plan to rescue our mate. They are not thinking, and it does not take a genius to work out — this is a trap.'

Marni's voice slices through the chaos in my head, sharp and impatient.

'Marni, quiet down, I am trying to focus and listen to the conversations around me.'

'Come on, do you think someone has enough brain cells to organise a rescue plan, one which includes you not fighting for your life?'

Her sarcasm curls through me. I shake my head, but I keep listening. I always listen to her, even when she's being a menace. And after a moment, her idea starts to take shape — dangerous, reckless, but logical. Whichever way this goes, I will have to fight for my life. I can either fight on my terms... or be captured, tortured, and dead before I ever reach Braven.

My stomach twists. My fingers tighten around my mug.

Enough. Time to interrupt the group and force this chaos into something resembling a plan.

TWO HOURS LATER — TWO HOURS OF CALMLY explaining my rescue plan while being drowned in a chorus of no's, are you insane, and that's far too dangerous — I finally have the assistance of the local wares and witches LJ introduced me to. Not approval. Not agreement. But assistance. I'll take it.

I've changed into clothes ready for fighting — well, more like armour disguised as clothing. Layers designed to protect vital organs and arteries. Practical. Uncomfortable. Necessary.

With Marni pushing me through a couple of quick practice shifts, I manage to shift back to human form with my clothing still intact. A small victory. I'll take that too.

With time to spare, I force myself to eat, then lie down for a short nap. My body rests. My mind doesn't.

"Misty, have you heard a word I have said?"

What...? Who? What?

I jerk upright and turn toward the unexpected male voice. It takes me a moment to place it — deep, warm, annoyingly amused. LJ's gorgeous brother, Jamie Jai.

Excitement bursts out of me before I can stop it. "What are you doing here, JJ?"

Before I can breathe, JJ wraps his arms around me, lifts me clean off the ground, and twirls me in circles like I'm a rag doll.

"Put me down before I throw up all over you," I grit out, clenching my teeth as my stomach lurches.

JJ laughs, the bastard. "Hey, Kitty girl. I heard from a little birdie you require a few more handsome, strong hands. So here I am."

"Oh, really. So where..." I glance around dramatically, "...are all the handsome, strong hands and more importantly, the bodies to go with the hands?"

He clutches his chest, lip pouting. "...You wound me, Miss Kitty. Ouch."

A laugh escapes me as I step back, keeping my eyes locked

on him. The room tilts slightly. The last thing I need is to vomit in front of everyone. If I do, they'll lock me in a broom closet before letting me near Braven.

I lift my hand, stopping JJ mid-stride. "Stop, JJ. I have to prepare myself."

His expression shifts — playfulness draining, concern sharpening. "Misty, you do know this mission is dangerous."

I nod, then whisper, "I know. However, JJ, it is the only way to rescue Braven. As time progresses, so are my memories, and I know I love him. He is my soulmate, and I need to protect him."

JJ doesn't hesitate. He pulls me into his arms, chin resting on top of my head, holding me like he's trying to anchor me to the earth.

"I am worried and concerned for you, Misty. We all are, especially LJ."

I melt into his warmth, letting myself breathe for a moment. "JJ, I love your sister as if she were mine. If I can protect you all, I will."

A female voice cuts through my mind, sharp and urgent. *'Misty. Come on, girl. It's time to go.'*

My stomach drops. My pulse spikes. I swallow down the nausea clawing up my throat.

With my hand protectively over my belly, I answer her.

'I just hope we are doing the right thing, Marni?'

'You are stronger than you think, Malisty. We will succeed.'

Her certainty settles over me like a cloak. Heavy. Comforting. Terrifying.

And then I exhale, because there's no turning back now.

Chapter Forty-Three
Misty

I START TO FEEL AS IF THE AIR IS THINNING, LIKE someone has cracked open a vacuum in the middle of the room. My lungs drag in shallow breaths that don't quite reach where they need to. Maybe it's the stuffiness of being packed into a room full of cat shifters... or maybe it's the fact that half the people in here could order my death with a single nod. Hard to tell which one is making my pulse throb in my throat.

I shift on the hard wooden seat, pretending I'm just trying to get comfortable. Really, I'm stalling. Delaying. Buying myself seconds I don't have. The chair creaks under me, loud enough that a few elders glance my way with polite, unsettling smiles.

I sit at a massive oval timber table — sixteen seats, all filled. All eyes on me. All smiles aimed at me. Shifters I'm internally terrified of... or paranoid about. Still working that one out.

What in the world am I doing, meeting the elders of Braven's family cat clan in one sitting? I shake my head slightly, because this — this — is the last thing I expected. Them welcoming me with open arms? Surreal doesn't even begin to cover it.

Three of the elders recognised me instantly. How, I have no clue. But they didn't hesitate to announce it to the room, their voices carrying like bells. Trepidation races through me. The plan to rescue Braven feels like it's seconds away from blowing up in my face.

I keep reminding myself to stay calm. Marni drilled it into me: if the elders suspect who I really am, stick to the story. My parents died in a car accident. I have no memory of clan life. No memory of being one of them.

Unease crawls through my body, prickling under my skin. It takes a while — too long — for the elders to accept my explanation. Marni was right, though. Eventually they nod, but their eyes stay sharp, probing. They know exactly who I am. And they keep circling back to the same questions, like wolves testing a fence for weak spots.

I have no memories of being a little girl surrounded by shifters. Only fragmented flashes of Braven and me as children. And I'm definitely not mentioning what Marni has started showing me — our past, our truth, the things buried so deep they ache.

With everything happening, maybe remembering would be smart. Maybe it would save my life. But right now, all I can do is answer their rapid-fire questions as truthfully as possible without giving away the parts that will get me killed.

When I mention putting myself through university and where I work, the elders beam at me, pleased with my achievements. Pride radiates off them like heat.

But then I mention the one thing they don't like — how I

know nothing about shifters. Their smiles falter. Their eyes narrow. And when I admit I've never shifted into my animal form, not once, not ever... disbelief ripples around the table.

"How can that be, young Malisty?" one elder demands.

I shrug lightly, keeping my voice steady. "I'm sorry; I really do not know much about my old life with my parents. I remember hearing a voice in my head as a child. My parents' reaction was to take me to see someone — at the time, I thought it was a doctor. Soon after the consultation, the voice stopped, leaving me feeling alone."

I meet each elder's gaze as I continue. "It wasn't until I was with Braven and he shifted into his animal form that I had any awareness of this world. He just about gave me a heart attack, finding a large black cat in the bathroom with me."

A few elders giggle, nodding knowingly. They don't seem to notice how carefully I'm dancing around the truth of my own shift.

"Malisty, since arriving back here in Lakes Entrance, have you been able to detect or hear your cat?" Master Layton asks.

I nod slowly. "Since I have arrived in Lakes Entrance... I have felt the presence of another being in my body, and I have been hearing her voice talking to me as if I am some old lost friend."

"Maybe young Malisty has to be near her kind to shift," Madam Georgina says brightly. "She is home now; we should be able to see her shift after all these years. It will be good to see her cat."

Her smile is too wide. Too knowing.

"Young Malisty," Master Tainer says, voice dropping into

something heavier, "why do I have the feeling there is a reason which has not been discussed — the reason for you to be here? If you are Braven's soulmate, then where is Braven? And why is he not here with you?"

My spine stiffens. Time to remain calm. Time to sound professional. Deep breath — here goes nothing.

I meet Master Tainer's eyes. "That is a very good question, Master Tainer. The main reason why I am here today is to do with Braven." I look around the room, meeting each elder's gaze. "Braven and I had been in Melbourne, where I live. Braven went downstairs in my building on his way to the shops. According to security, he was taken by force from the building car park."

The room erupts.

"What?"

"Who would do this?"

"Do you know who has taken him?"

I let them speak, let the panic build. Then I steady myself.

"Ladies and gentlemen, I have since learned the responsible person — or I should say persons — are—"

"Who would do such a vile thing?" someone snaps, cutting me off.

I scan the elders. "I don't know this person personally, but I have since learned that Braven's ex-fiancé is involved."

A sharp gasp. I turn toward the source.

"That two-faced bitch. What does she want with Braven?"

Ah. A clan member who is not a fan of Liasa. Good to know.

Another voice rises from the opposite side of the table.

"Malisty, you said persons. Who else is involved in taking our future alpha?" Madam Georgina demands.

I straighten, voice clear. "Brian O'Geary."

The room freezes. The air thickens. And for the first time since walking in, the elders stop smiling.

Chapter Forty-Four
Braven

Darkness surrounds me. Thick. Heavy. Suffocating. I can't tell if it's day or night, or if time has stopped altogether. My face throbs, but it's not just my face — my whole body is a map of pain, every inch marked, every line burning.

What in the hell is going on?

I push at my memory, trying to force something — anything — into focus. Where am I? Who did this? Where is Misty? Is she safe?

A faint brush of air ghosts across my skin, and goosebumps erupt along my flesh. Goosebumps. That shouldn't be possible. Not unless—

What the... I'm naked.

Why am I naked?

I squeeze my eyes tighter, then force them open. The lids feel like they're glued together. I blink, once, twice, trying to clear the wetness clinging to my lashes. Pain spikes as my dry tongue drags across swollen lips, catching on something split and raw. The metallic tang hits instantly.

Blood. My blood.

It takes me a moment to realise it's dripping into my eyes, warm and slow. My eyes don't want to stay open anyway. They're swollen. Heavy. Bruised.

A pathetic attempt to wiggle my toes sends agony shooting up my legs. My groin — fuck. Excruciating doesn't even cover it.

Fragments of memory slam into me, jagged and bright.

Oh shit.

That fucking bitch.

Liasa. She's responsible.

The overload of images, the stress, the pain — everything blurs. My senses dim, fade, tilt sideways.

If I didn't know any better, I'd say I'm about to pass out.

"**WAKE UP, YOU PIECE OF SHIT. IT'S TIME TO GO.**"

My father's voice — angry, venomous — cuts through the haze a second before something hard and solid cracks against my body. Once. Twice. Again. The blows barely register through the blanket of pain already smothering me, but each one still sends a dull shockwave through my bones.

I drag in a breath, and a pungent stench fills my nostrils — sweat, blood, rot, and something sour that can only belong to the pathetic excuse of a man who fathered me. And Liasa. She's here too. I can smell her perfume under the filth. Sweet. Fake. Poisonous.

I breathe in again, deeper this time, and something else threads through the air. Faint. Delicious. Impossible. My mate is here. Oh fuck no. Misty can't be here. Wherever here is. No.

My heart tries to launch itself out of my chest, but I clamp down on it, forcing the rhythm to slow. If they sense the spike — if they smell the shift in my scent — they'll know something's wrong. I have to stay calm. I have to think. I have to figure out what in the hell Misty is doing anywhere near this place.

I pry my battered eyelids open again. The world swims, blurs, then sharpens just enough to reveal two figures standing over me — shapes I know too well. Brian. Liasa. The pair of them radiate smugness and cruelty like it's perfume.

If I survive this, they'll be dead by the end of the day. Or night. Or whatever the fuck time it is. They'll pay for what they've done to me. To the clan. To Misty.

I've heard their plans. Their greed. Their stupidity. They'll destroy the clan and not give a single fuck who gets caught in the fallout. They've already stolen clan finances. They're planning to run. Leave the clan open for war. Wolves circling like vultures. And Brian — my father — has already opened the door for them.

Fucking bastard.

With a croak, I manage, "What is so important that you require my presence?"

A boot lifts. Slow. Deliberate. My brain screams at my body to move, but I'm too slow. The steel-capped toe slams into my ribs, sending me sliding across the rough floor. My head cracks against the wall, stars exploding behind my eyes.

Ahhh fuck. That's another rib gone.

I glare at the pathetic man who calls himself my father and spit a glob of blood at his feet. It lands with a wet slap, and for a moment, the room tilts again.

Then something registers. I'm not chained. Well. That explains why I moved so far.

I suck in a sharp breath and try again. "What is going on, Brian? And where am I?"

He sneers. "Braven, you are too soft for your own good." He shakes his head, glancing between me and Liasa. "It seems the elders found out you've been staying here for a few days and want to speak with you. So get off the fucking floor and get dressed."

Something's off. Brian following orders? That's new.

Interesting.

"Hold on, Brian. One, I require a shower. And two, some clothes would be appropriate."

He lunges at me again, but this time I'm ready. I roll just enough to avoid the steel toe aimed at my ribs. Pain screams through my side, but I grit my teeth.

Fuck, that was close.

"Watch it, Brian," I rasp. "You don't want to leave any more bruising, do you?"

"Get the fuck dressed, Braven, or you'll be leaving here in a body bag instead." He kicks again, aiming for my head. I dodge, barely.

I spot a pile of filthy clothes nearby. I reach for them with stiff fingers, each movement a fresh wave of agony. Pulling them on is torture. My ribs scream. My limbs shake. My breath stutters.

And Liasa... I can feel her eyes crawling over my skin. If she comes close enough, I'll snap her neck. I don't care how broken I am.

I take longer than I want to dress, but eventually I manage to shove my feet into my shoes. Liasa opens the door and turns her back to me. Idiot. Never turn your back on the enemy.

Brian's voice snaps like a whip. "Don't even think about it, Braven. Liasa is about to go into the clearing and fight in a death challenge."

My head whips toward him so fast pain shoots down my neck.

Death challenge?

Say what?

Who?

Then it hits me.

Misty.

Oh fuck.

NO.

My vision tunnels. My pulse spikes. My cat claws at the inside of my skin, frantic, enraged, desperate to break free. The scent I caught earlier — faint, terrified, determined — wasn't a hallucination. It was her. My mate. My Misty.

She's here.

She's in danger.

She's about to fight a death challenge.

A roar builds in my chest, low and feral, vibrating through my cracked ribs. I swallow it down before it escapes, before

Brian notices, before I give away the one thing that will get her killed instantly.

I push myself upright, every muscle screaming, every bone protesting. My legs wobble. My vision flickers. But I stay standing.

Because Misty is here.

And I will crawl through fire before I let anything happen to her.

Brian smirks, thinking he's won. Thinking I'm broken. Thinking I'm too weak to do anything.

He has no idea.

I take one step toward the door. Pain lances through my side. I grit my teeth and take another.

Liasa glances back, her eyes gleaming with sick satisfaction. "Don't worry, Braven. I'll make sure she dies quickly."

My vision goes red.

I don't remember crossing the room. I don't remember the snarl ripping from my throat. I don't remember slamming my shoulder into the doorframe as I shove past them.

All I know is this: Misty is out there.

Alone.

Facing a death challenge meant to kill her. And I am coming for her. Broken or not. Bleeding or not. Half-dead or not. I will reach her. I will protect her. I will tear apart anyone who touches her.

Even if it kills me.

Chapter Forty-Five
Misty

What in the hell was I thinking?

The clearing feels too open, too exposed, too bright under the midday sun. Every rustle of leaves sounds like a threat. Every shifting body around me feels like a predator waiting for me to slip. It amazes me — truly amazes me — that the elders agreed to let me participate in the death challenge. But then again, they don't like Liasa. They want her out of the pack, out of the district, out of existence if possible. And Brian — the so-called alpha — well, chances are I'll have to fight him too.

If he kills me, my replacement can step in and finish the job. JJ volunteered, bless his cute pussycat arse. But still — am I going to survive the first death challenge?

As far as the elders and local shifters know, I haven't shifted. So they assume I'll die anyway. Geez, thanks a bunch — the confidence and love are overwhelming. At least by orchestrating the death challenge, Braven will be delivered here to the clearing.

'You will be fine, Malisty. We can do this. I will make sure to protect our young and fight for our lives. You know how to fight in human form, and you know how to shift. Allow me to take over when we are in cat form, and we will survive. We will win,' Marni announces, full of attitude and claws.

'Marni, please take care of us and avoid taking unnecessary risks. Liasa is out to win and cheat, so keep your senses open,' I plead.

A breeze brushes my cheek, carrying the scent of pine, earth, and too many shifters. I sense LJ move up behind me, and I force myself not to whirl around and attack. My nerves are shot. My heart is racing against my ribs like it's trying to escape.

"Hey, girl. How are you doing over here?" LJ murmurs as she slips an arm around me. My body instantly calms at her touch, like she's grounding me to the earth.

"A little better now you're standing with me. How is JJ? I'm so sorry he was roped into all this. The last thing I want is for him to fight on my behalf against Brian and Liasa."

"Misty, stop it. My brother is a big boy now. Plus, he's an excellent fighter. Do you know he also fights in those underground fight clubs? He's quite good, you know," LJ says proudly.

Hmm. With a nod, I reply, "At least one of us has seen action and lived to tell the story. I just wish I had more time and practice. JJ has been busy showing me some fighting moves, including protection and dodging. I have to remember to use them and not get myself killed."

"Misty, you can do this," she says with absolute certainty. "I have some news — some of the other members of my parents' clan have already detected Braven with their magical abilities. So we know he is alive and here. The only thing is that he is in pain. Those mongrels have done a number on him. So far, your plan has succeeded, and Braven is still alive. Ahh, and speaking of Braven, he is moving this way."

Huh? I must be blocking Braven with all my stressing; I haven't sensed his approach. I turn my head and open my senses until I find my mate.

Oh. My. God. What have they done to him?

His pain hits me like a punch to the chest. His suffering bleeds into my bones. Those animals will pay for what they've done to my soulmate.

I feel Braven at the edge of my mind, and relief floods me. Our connection snaps open, warm and familiar, and I let him in.

'Braven. It is good to see you're still alive. I have been so worried about you.'

His voice is strained, ragged. *'Misty. What in the world are you doing here? You know this is a trap, don't you?'*

'Yes, Braven,' I reply with an eye roll he can probably feel. *'We know that. We already know Liasa and Brian have been stealing money from the clan, and the elders are not happy about it. Once they found out you had been forcibly taken, including other details of rather disturbing pieces of information, they were all too willing to sacrifice me in a death*

challenge to make sure you continued to live and become the next alpha.'

'Baby, I love you so much. But what about our babies in the fight?'

'My cat will protect us. She is ready to go all out and seek revenge. She is one protective pussycat.'

'Misty, Brian wants you. Liasa wants you dead. Chances are they will try to kill me before the challenge is over.'

'Don't worry about anyone trying to kill you. The elders and LJ's people are here to make sure you survive. As for me, well, I have JJ as backup.'

'Back up? What do you mean, JJ is your backup? Usually, the only backup is when one challenger dies and their second can step in and continue the fight if the elders agree.'

'Well, hopefully, JJ's services will not be required. Now I know you are here, the elders will make sure to move you to a safe location, and you'll be well protected.'

A pause. A shift. A tightening of fear. 'Misty, what are you not saying?'

I swallow. Hard. 'Braven, I have to prepare myself mentally. So I had better go. Plus, I have to start some stretches and warm up.'

'Baby, I do not want you fighting. You are not a fighter. You can barely shift for fuck's sake. If only I—'

Anger flares hot and sharp. For goodness sake, my so-called mate is demonstrating he does not have faith in me. Well, I am going to show him.

'Braven, stop it. I can take care of myself. Now go with the elders and make sure to clean up and start healing. And remember... I love you.'

Even though Braven is concerned for my welfare and has trust issues with my new abilities, I still love him.

'Baby, why does that sound like a goodbye?'

'It is not goodbye, but a promise. I will be with you soon. Okay!'

'I love you, too. Please be careful.'

I nod, turn away from Braven's direction, and block him from talking to me. I have to concentrate. Marni has a few more lessons for me to learn before I fight anyone.

I watch LJ's back as she approaches JJ. They're talking fast, hands moving, tension radiating off them. Strategies. Contingencies. Backup plans. Good. They'd better watch over Braven and keep him safe for me.

'We will win, Malisty.' Arhh shit. Marni's voice makes me jump a foot off the ground. *'Do not doubt our ability.'*

I exhale, roll my shoulders back, and step toward the centre of the clearing.

The death challenge is coming. And I am not running.

Chapter Forty-Six
Misty

I STAND IN THE CLEARING, THE DRY EARTH CRACKING beneath my boots, the air thick with dust and anticipation. Shifters and witches ring the arena in a wide circle, their murmurs low, tense, hungry. My right foot taps the ground in a steady rhythm, the only outward sign of the storm building inside me.

JJ explained the rules — well, the lack of them. As soon as Liasa steps into the arena, all bets are off. No countdown. No warning. No mercy.

I'm grateful Braven has been taken away to be medically checked. One less person to protect. One less distraction. One less reason for my heart to leap out of my chest.

My senses prickle. A vile presence slithers into the clearing. No — two. My palms itch. My skin tingles. The fine hairs at the back of my neck rise like they're trying to escape my body.

Liasa steps into the clearing with a feral death stare aimed straight at me.

Wow. Is she trying to scare me? Intimidate me?

Cute.

I clear my mind, pushing away the whispers, the crowd, the distant rustle of leaves. I focus on her. The way she moves. The way her weight shifts. The way her lips curl like she's already tasting victory.

What in the hell was Braven thinking, getting involved with this slut? She struts like she's God's gift to men. To me, she looks like a skinny, long blonde-haired skank with delusions of grandeur.

But I can't underestimate her. One mistake, and she'll rip my throat out.

JJ's lessons. Marni's instincts. My own stubborn will to live. I pull them all close, wrapping them around me like armour.

I stay light on my feet. My heart refuses to listen, pounding frantically against my ribs, its tattooing beat loud in my ears.

Slow breath in. Eyes locked on the blonde bitch.

I need to remain in human form for as long as possible. Let her think I'm weak. Let her think I'm mostly human. Let her underestimate me.

We circle each other. Again. And again. Dust swirls around our feet. The crowd leans in. Liasa's eyes narrow, calculating.

Does she think if we circle long enough, I'll get dizzy and fall over? Who knows what goes on in that empty skull.

'Malisty, I have been focusing on the bitch. It did not take me long to work out Liasa is indeed pregnant. I don't know if her animal would be able to protect the cub. But then, this is a death challenge. And sadly, the innocent little thing will die, along with its mother.'

My stomach drops.

'Oh, no. Why did you have to tell me that, Marni? We can't kill her, knowing she is pregnant?'

'Why? She knows you are pregnant and is determined to kill you and our cubs.'

'But—'

'No, Malisty. Do not look upon her as a human, for she is not. This shifter is a vicious bitch who will do anything to move ahead in the pack. She would kill our innocent cubs without hesitation.'

I swallow hard.

Okay. I remind myself I am a shifter fighting another shifter who wants me dead.

Kill the bitch before she kills me. Yeah. I'll work on that as soon as I remove my morals from my humanity.

Liasa smirks, her voice dripping with sarcasm. "Are you really a shifter? You seem more human than shifter. So I'll begin the fight in human form, as it's been said you haven't managed to shift. But as soon as I shift, all bets are off."

I detect a shift in her stance. A tightening. A twitch. Oh good. The bitch is about to make her move.

'Yes, she is. Now prepare yourself. Strike her before she makes contact. You know how to protect yourself. JJ has shown you moves to incapacitate someone. NOW DO IT,' Marni screams.

Her voice nearly knocks me off balance.

'Shit, Marni, not so loud.'

'Sorry,' she whispers — then shrieks, *'watch out!'*

Liasa lunges.

At the last possible second, I sidestep and swivel away, feeling the breeze of her fist as it misses my head by a hair. I spin, faster than she expects, my knee lifting, my hand reaching.

My fingers clamp around her arm. Hard. I yank her toward me. She's stunned — good. She expected a scared little human. Not me.

My knee slams into her kidney. A sickening oomph bursts from her lips.

Before she can recover, my other hand thrusts upward, striking her bare throat. The impact is brutal. Her windpipe collapses under my palm. Her head snaps back with a crack.

She drops. Slowly. Like a puppet with its strings cut.

I step back, breathing hard. She clutches her throat, eyes wide, panicked. She tries to breathe. She can't. Her face reddens, then purples. Her fingers claw at her neck, desperate.

She reaches toward me — pleading. I stare down at her. I will not help her. I will not end it quickly. She tortured Braven. She tried to kill my cubs. She walked into a death challenge. This is justice.

JJ's words echo in my mind — strike fast, incapacitate, end it.

Well, I did.

Liasa's body convulses. Her eyes glaze. Her hand falls limp.

Silence ripples through the clearing.

I take several steps back, turning my back on her corpse. My gaze locks on Brian. He smiles. A slow, crawling, skin-peeling smile. He lifts his bulky hands and begins to clap.

Slow. Mocking. Deadly.

Behind me, I hear Liasa's final, rattling attempt at breath.

Then nothing. Shit. Liasa is dead.

Now comes the next stage of the plan — if I live long enough to see it.

Brian's eyes gleam with something feral. Something cruel. Something hungry.

The air thickens. The crowd shifts uneasily. Magic crackles. The earth seems to hold its breath. Brian takes one step forward. Then another.

And I know — something terrible is about to happen.

CHAPTER FORTY-SEVEN
BRAVEN

I RUSH AS QUICKLY AS I CAN THROUGH A MEDICAL, forcing my body to shift back and forth several times. Bones crack, reform, crack again. Muscles tear and knit. Skin ripples. My cat snarls inside me, furious at the damage, furious at the weakness, furious that Misty is out there alone.

I encourage my enhanced healing abilities to kick-start and repair my broken bones and battered body.

I don't know what's worse — the pain inflicted by the injuries or the agony of shifting to heal them. My throat is raw from each painful growl and scream, each time I shift, each time another bone rebreaks and begins to reset. Every shift feels like being skinned alive and stitched back together with barbed wire. All I know is I do not want to do that again in a hurry. It's too bloody painful.

Within twenty minutes — though it feels like hours — I'm showered, dressed in clean clothing, and sitting at a small table. I scoff down a large rare steak and vegetables, barely chewing, washing it down with juice and a few pain-medicated tablets prescribed especially for shifters.

The tablets scrape down my throat like gravel. I gag. I force them down anyway. I need to be back in the clearing. I have to be there for my mate. I cannot let her fight to the death without me being there for support.

With LJ by my side, I swallow another mouthful of juice, trying to drown the damn pills. The doctor refused to let me leave unless I took them — more like horse tablets, by the size of them.

Once the doctor is satisfied with my healing progress, I manage to convince LJ to take me back to the clearing.

I might look okay to the doctor, but realistically, my body is ready to collapse into a heap and sleep for a week. My ribs ache. My muscles tremble. My vision flickers at the edges. But none of that matters.

Misty is fighting.

HOLY SHIT.

I don't know whether to be stunned, impressed, proud, or shocked by my beautiful soulmate's moves and abilities.

I didn't know she was capable of such techniques. I shouldn't be surprised — she protected herself against three wolves on her first day in Lakes Entrance. She avoided being dragged back to their boss. She survived that.

But still...

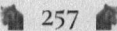

I feel like a piece of shit for doubting her before her big fight.

My eyes move back to Liasa. Her human form is losing the fight to live. Her body convulses once, twice, then struggles for a final breath that never comes. Her chest stills. Her eyes glaze.

Relief floods me.

That damn bitch is dead.

Should I be worried that Misty let her die slowly instead of delivering a merciful strike?

Strangely enough... no.

I am proud of my soulmate. She survived the first death challenge. She fought like a warrior. She fought like a queen.

However, this challenge is far from over. Brian is up to something, and I cannot determine what it is. His scent is wrong — too calm, too controlled. His heartbeat is steady. His posture relaxed. That alone terrifies me.

I keep myself hidden among the shadows, protected by LJ and her family's magic. The last thing I want is to distract Misty. I would only fail her if I stepped into the clearing. My body is too weak to fight, let alone shift.

I watch her. My mate. My fierce, stubborn, breathtaking mate.

She stands tall, shoulders squared, chin lifted, facing Brian like she's ready to take on the world. Dust swirls around her feet. Her hair whips in the wind. Her eyes burn with determination and something darker — justice.

The crowd murmurs.

Magic crackles.

The earth itself seems to hold its breath.

Brian's slow clapping echoes through the clearing, each clap a threat, a promise, a countdown.

LJ grips my arm, her magic tightening around me like a shield. "Stay back," she whispers. "He's dangerous. More dangerous than you think."

I know. I can feel it. Brian's smile widens, cruel and hungry. He steps forward. The crowd recoils.

Misty doesn't move. She doesn't flinch. She doesn't blink. Gods, she's magnificent.

I focus on her, praying to every deity our people have ever worshipped. I hope — I pray — that we both survive the night.

Because the real fight is about to begin.

Chapter Forty-Eight
Misty

I FEEL MARNI HISS AND CLAW IN MY MIND, PACING like a caged predator. She wants out. She wants to shift. She wants to tear into the bad man standing across from us. Her fury vibrates through my bones, hot and electric.

Over the last few days, Marni has opened up my memories, peeling back layers I didn't even know existed. She's shown me my past, the history I once had with this pack. Especially the bad, ugly memories that contain Brian. I don't know how Braven survived living under that man's roof for so many years. If I had been Braven, I would have killed Brian years ago.

With Marni's ability to look into others' minds, we've started to see the truth — the sad, horrible truth of what that man has done to this clan and its members. The manipulation. The cruelty. The secrets. The rot.

Brian is still clapping and smiling — or is that sneering? Hard to tell. His expression is a twisted mix of pride and malice.

His voice cuts through my thoughts like a blade. "Well done. I wanted Liasa dead. However, I was not expecting the bitch's death to be — so quick."

Whoa. What?

Brian was expecting me to succeed? Yeah right.

He's trying to fill me with false bravado. Trying to lull me into thinking the death challenge is over. But I know better. This is only the beginning.

"Your fighting skills are beyond anything I had ever hoped for. Well done, young Misty. For a financial planner and broker, your physical aptitude far outstands that of most of these pathetic men in this clan pack."

His words ripple through the clearing like poison. I feel the tension spike among the men standing around the arena. A few callous whispers drift through the air. Brian has said too much. He's stirring trouble. He wants chaos.

Hang on — that's exactly what he's aiming for. He wants the pack to turn on itself so he can escape. I don't think so, Mr Bad-Mean-Man-Brian the Soon-to-Be Ex-Alpha.

"Brian, we have never met," I say loudly, clearly, projecting my voice across the clearing. The pack members fall silent. No one apart from the elders knows who I truly am, and we agreed to keep it that way. "And yet I know enough to know you are stealing from your own clan."

The whispers stop instantly. Different clan members look from one another, then at Brian, then at me.

"Stealing the clan's finances so you can leave them bankrupt and allow the rogue wolves to step in and take over. Sorry to disappoint you, Brian, but your days as alpha are over."

"What is the meaning of this, alpha?" someone shouts.

Another voice rises, angrier. "Are the accusations this stranger is making true? Have you been stealing the clan's money for your own gain? Leaving us at the mercy of the wolves?"

The murmurs return — louder, sharper, turning against him.

Brian takes a step back. Then another. He realises he's in trouble.

"Where are you moving off to, Brian?" I ask, stepping forward. "I think the clan and the elders deserve to know the truth, don't you? How you've been fucking your own son's fiancé — let me rephrase that — Braven's ex-fiancé, Liasa. Stealing what you both could from not just your own family but the clan."

Several pack members move toward him, slow and deliberate. The circle tightens.

"Kidnapping and torturing your own son. Why? So Liasa could continue raping him, milking him for his seed. When you both knew he is soulmated to another. Or did it get you off watching your sons fuck her in front of you?"

Even from across the clearing, I see Brian's eyes widen. His anger spikes. His scent shifts — fear, rage, humiliation.

Hmmm. Interesting. Brian didn't like seeing Liasa fuck his sons. The bastard doesn't like to share.

"Arranging for the two of you to leave and travel overseas. Only Liasa wasn't going with you, was she? You planned to kill her before leaving the country. Dump her body. Fly away with all the money."

Brian's skin tone shifts — red, then pale, then a sickly grey. Another nerve hit.

The pack closes in around him, no longer his followers. No longer his slaves. They are now his enemies.

His face turns white. He knows. His number is up.

"What do you have to say for yourself, Brian? Why did you turn your back on your own people? Why open the door and allow the wolves free range of your territory?"

He shakes his head, breath hitching. "No. No. Sh-She... She is wrong. I did not do these things — "

An elder's voice booms across the clearing. "No, Brian. We also have proof. We, as the pack elders, decree you are no longer the alpha of the Lakes Entrance Black Panther Clan. With the multitude of charges brought forward, we demand death. Yours. For what you have done. Your betrayal. You were sending us to our deaths. It is fitting we do the same to you. Clan members — shift and hand out our kind of clan justice to the one who betrayed us all."

Several elders echo, "May the gods have mercy on your soul."

Before I can process what's happening, the pack shifts as one — an explosion of fur, claws, and snarls. They leap toward Brian, burying him under a mass of attacking cats.

His screams rip through the clearing. Begging. Pleading. Shrieking.

The growls drown him out. The tearing. The ripping. The wet sounds of flesh being shredded.

Bile rises in my throat. The scent of blood fills the air — thick, metallic, suffocating.

My vision blurs. My knees buckle. Just as the world tilts,

strong arms wrap around me — warm, familiar, trembling with exhaustion.

Braven.

I turn my head into his chest, away from the carnage.

Where did Braven come from? Is my last thought before the darkness pulls me under.

Chapter Forty-Nine
Braven

Just for five minutes, leave me the fuck alone.

I knew the day would come. But come on... My mate needs me. My cubs need me. And Misty still hasn't woken up.

Shit.

She should have by now. The local shifter doctor said she'd be awake within the hour. It's been longer. Too long. My nerves are shredded. My cat is pacing inside me, snarling, demanding I do something — anything — to protect her.

I look down at my beautiful unconscious mate. Misty's breathing is steady, but too shallow for my liking. Her skin is warm, but not warm enough. My heart nearly stopped when she collapsed in my arms at the death challenge. One second, she was standing strong, fierce, victorious. The next — gone. Limp. Unresponsive.

The sound of another loud round of knocking against my front door grates on my nerves.

Shit.

Now I find myself in the position of unofficial alpha of the Lakes Entrance Black Panther Clan, and suddenly everyone has crawled out of the woodwork to burden me with their troubles. Well, they can bloody well wait. I'm not doing a damn thing until I know my mate and cubs are safe.

Cubs. Three of them!

I can feel them — tiny sparks of life, warm and bright, curled inside Misty's womb.

Mine. Ours. My chest tightens with a fierce, primal love.

All I need now is for my mate to wake up.

Another knock. Louder. More insistent.

What do I have betas and omegas for if they're not going to do their bloody job?

I shake my head, still unable to believe Misty agreed to go into a death challenge while carrying our cubs. Silly woman. Brave woman. Reckless woman. Just wait until she wakes up — I'll place her over my knee and tan her gorgeous backside.

The knocking becomes pounding, followed by the angry voice of my little brother. "Open the fucking door, Braven. Where is she?"

Of course. Marcus.

I pause mid-step, looking back at Misty. She's still asleep, peaceful in a way that terrifies me. I turn and walk down the hallway toward the front entrance.

"Braven, let me in, now!" Marcus yells.

Within seconds, I yank the door open, blocking the doorway with my body.

Marcus stands there, eyes wild, face blotchy with rage and grief. "Bring her out, Braven. She killed my mate. She deserves to die. She killed my cub."

Oh shit.

Right.

Liasa had managed to get herself pregnant. The only question was — who was the unlucky father?

Using my alpha calm, I say, "Marcus, you need to back off and calm down. Or I will use my alpha authority and make you. The choice is yours."

His features shift — rage, confusion, pain — until finally he looks me in the eyes again.

"Braven... I would like to speak with Misty."

"No. Misty is still sleeping, Marcus. And why in the hell are you calling Liasa your mate? She was still fucking our father right up until the death challenge."

He shakes his head violently. "No, Braven. Liasa said I was her only lover. I have been for the last three months."

I almost laugh. Almost. Did he not witness that bitch rape me. Did he miss when our father fucked her in the bathroom?

"Oh, Marcus. Your so-called beloved was still fucking our father. And she drugged me so she could fuck me in front of him. Your girlfriend was raping me while torturing me in that basement. Our father and your girlfriend kept me prisoner — drugged and tied up."

His face crumples.

My stupid, naive little brother believed everything Liasa told him. Now he's left to pick up the pieces.

A tear slides down his cheek. "I loved her, man. She was my mate."

"Really? So you both mated and gave each other the mate bites, just as Misty and I have?"

"Well... no. Her bite never took." He frowns. "I can't work it out. I did everything right, but our mate bites never took."

Poor bastard.

He had it bad for the little bitch.

"Marcus, did it ever occur to you that Liasa might have been mated to someone else? Which might be why she never fell pregnant to me?"

Not reminding him that I was already mated to Misty. The pack doesn't know Misty is really Malisty — my childhood soulmate.

"What? No. That can't be right. She would have said something."

"Really? So Liasa explained how she was having sex with me and our father while she was fucking you?"

Marcus's face twists, but not with understanding — with outrage.

"No. She said I was her only lover."

Of course he believes that. Of course he does. His love for the she-bitch is blind.

Marcus has always been desperate for someone — anyone — to choose him. Liasa played him like a fiddle.

"Marcus," I say slowly, deliberately, "do you think your scent was the only male scent I detected on her? Why do you think I removed everything from my house? The bitch tainted everything with each of her lovers."

He shakes his head violently, refusing to accept it. His denial is almost childish — stubborn, blind, pathetic.

"No. I don't believe you."

Of course, he doesn't. He never believes me until the truth smacks him in the face and knocks him flat.

"Go speak with the elders," I say, keeping my tone even. "They'll explain everything. Liasa was planted as a spy. To infiltrate our clan and learn our secrets."

His jaw clenches. His nostrils flare. His eyes dart away — guilt, confusion, fear — then snap back to me with renewed anger.

"No. That's not true."

He's clinging to the fantasy like it's the only thing keeping him upright.

"Go speak with the elders, Marcus."

"Misty still killed Liasa, Braven. I want justice."

There it is. The real reason he's here. Not grief. Not confusion. Revenge.

"No, Marcus. You know the rules. Once a death challenge has been called and won, you cannot seek retribution on the victor." I place my hand on his shoulder, squeezing gently — a warning disguised as comfort. "If Misty hadn't killed Liasa, then Liasa would have slaughtered Misty and my cubs."

His head snaps up so fast I hear the crack of his neck. "Cubs? Is Misty pregnant with your cubs? Twins or something?"

I hold his gaze. "Yes. Or something. It's early days, but yes — my soulmate is carrying my cubs."

His face crumples. Not with joy. Not with understanding. With betrayal.

"Why, Braven? Why did Liasa do this to me? To us?"

He still thinks this is about him. He still thinks he was the victim of a tragic love story instead of a manipulative spy who used him like a pawn.

"Marcus," I say, voice low, steady, "Liasa was a spy. Some of our men are investigating who sent her. The question is whether our father befriended her first... or whether she befriended him to learn our finances and clan secrets."

He staggers back a step, shaking his head. "No. No, she wouldn't... she wouldn't do that. She loved me."

"She loved no one," I say bluntly. "She used you. She used all of us."

"I... I'm sorry, Braven. I'd better go."

"That might be wise. Go speak to the elders. You need closure."

He nods, but it's mechanical — like his body is moving without his mind. He turns and walks away, shoulders slumped, steps heavy, but there's something else in his posture too.

Resentment. Wounded pride. A dangerous mix. I watch him go, my jaw tight, my cat pacing beneath my skin.

Marcus is a fool. A grieving fool. A fool who refuses to believe the truth even when it's shoved down his throat. And fools are unpredictable.

I hope the stupid little idiot doesn't try to hurt my mate. Because if he does, I will end his pathetic life.

Brother or not — if anyone threatens my soulmate, they forfeit their life.

Chapter Fifty
Misty

Twelve Months Later

Hmmm. Now, this is what I enjoy...

Braven's hand glides along my skin, slow and deliberate, leaving a trail of heat in its wake. My breath catches before I can stop it. Even after everything — the chaos, the cubs, the sleepless nights — he still knows exactly how to touch me, how to wake every nerve in my body.

Yes, officially my husband.

I still can't believe it sometimes — the secret wedding he arranged with LJ's help, tucked away on her family's property, five months after the death challenge. A quiet ceremony, just us, just love, just the promise of a future we nearly lost.

"Hmmmm. And where do you think you're going, my husband?"

He freezes for half a heartbeat — caught — then groans softly against my neck.

"Good morning, my beautiful wife and mate. How are you feeling? Think we might have time for a quickie before anyone interrupts us?"

I laugh, low and warm. "Just for you... I think we should take advantage before someone comes knocking."

Braven doesn't need to be told twice. In one smooth, hungry movement, he rolls me beneath him, my back sinking into the mattress as he lifts my legs, settling between them with the kind of confidence only a bonded mate can have. His eyes darken, pupils blown wide, drinking me in like I'm the only thing in his world.

His breath brushes my inner thigh. His hands grip my hips. His whole body hums with that familiar, possessive heat. And gods... the way he looks at me — like I'm his entire universe — still steals the air from my lungs.

"Hmm. Yummy and just for me," Braven manages to say, as he makes himself more comfortable until his mouth is covering my swollen lips and his tongue slides in and out of my clenching wet channel, tasting my warm juices with each swipe and thrust of his tongue. He lifts his head slightly and manages to murmur against my weeping flesh."Baby, I want you to come in my mouth. I have missed your pussy, and no one is going to stop me from eating you out."

Well, now. I am not going to argue with him there. I love it when he goes to town on me.

First, I feel his tongue penetrate as deep as it can go before he sucks on my swollen flesh.

'Oh, Gods, yes. More. Right there. More,' I scream in my mind as I feel his fingers introduced to the mix along with his tongue and teeth as he starts to nip at my sensitive clit.

'Hold on tight, baby. You are going to fly off the bed before I am finished,' Braven informs me through our mind link.

I attempt to roll my hips and push my desperate sex-deprived pussy, further into his mouth. Oh, gods, I need this. Since the wedding and the birth of the cubs, our sex life has gone out of the window. As Braven has found, becoming the alpha, our lives are no longer our own.

"Baby, stop moving, or I will not let you come."

I pause and groan, feeling frustrated when Braven removes his mouth from my sex.

'Nooo. Come back,' my mind pleads, *"Braven, please. Please more. I need more. I need to feel you, baby. Please,"* I pant and demand.

I might start to cry, as my eyes mist up with the loss of Braven's talented mouth and fingers from my body.

I open my eyes, look down, and watch as Braven maneuvers back up my body, taking one of my legs with him, opening me right up for his penetration, and I notice the glint in his eyes.

I start to move my mouth to ask him what is going on. When Braven thrusts powerfully forward, impaling me on his solid, hard length, knocking the wind out of my lungs, stretching my underused muscles.

Braven rushes and ploughs through my tight channel. I can sense he is fighting to remain in control against my tight weeping pulsing flesh. I just hope I have been screaming my pleasure within my head and not out loud. Braven grunts and moans his, at the same time, hearing his sexual thoughts through our mind link.

'Fuuuuuck, Misty. It's been tooo looong,' Braven says between thrusts. *'I do not think I will last much longer. Do you think you will be able to come on my dick soon?'*

Braven demands on his next thrust, feeling his cock grow and pulse within me. I manage to reach down between our bodies, and with my hand, I start to rub and circle my swollen bundle of nerves, just the right way, enhancing my orgasm, I know is only a few more well-placed thrusts away.

'Oh, fuck, yes. Right there, Braven. Harder baby. Faster. Right there.' I repeat my mantra, with each powerful thrust, at the same time, my hand is kept busy stroking my clit, just right.

I lift my other leg, making my body open up more, allowing Braven deeper penetration, hitting all those delicious places only he can reach, and touch.

'Yes. Yes. That's it. Baby, I'm coming. I'm coming.' Braven screams through our mind link.

I am soon feeling his hot seed hit my inner walls, triggering off my own orgasm, as my eyes roll back in my head from the overload of sexual pleasure my mate has caused.

After a few minutes — or an hour, who knows — my brain finally kicks back into gear enough to realise Braven is plastered on top of me, all heavy muscle and heat, and my hand is still wedged between our sweaty bodies.

In between rushed breaths, I manage, "Ah, baby... I need you to move... my hand is stuck, and... you're starting to get heavy."

Braven grunts near my ear, the sound low and delicious, before he tries — and fails — to shift his big muscly body.

"Shit. Sorry, baby. I think you nearly killed me," he groans. With another heave, he manages to lift himself off me, sliding away from between my thighs before leaning down to kiss me again — slow, warm, lingering.

I melt into it... until he pauses. His head tilts slightly to the side. That look. That damn look. Someone is speaking to him through the clan-pack mind link.

"Damn it," he mutters. "I have to go, Misty."

I sigh, brushing my fingers along his jaw. "Okay, honey. Don't forget, I have to head into the city today and drop off those financial reports and attend the council meeting."

"Really? I thought that was tomorrow."

With a small shake of my head, I reply, "Sadly, no. It's today. I'd better get up, shower, and dress."

I lift my head, and Braven leans down, giving me a gentle kiss — the kind that always leaves me wanting more, the kind that promises more later.

"I love you, baby."

"I love you, too. I'll be back before you know it."

"Are the kids going with you?"

I turn my head toward the bedside clock.

Damn.

It's earlier than I thought. No wonder the kids aren't awake yet. At least this way I can shower without three little munchkins barging in and demanding to join me.

I look back at my sexy husband and smile. Maybe... maybe I can entice him back into bed for round two.

"No. I'll be quicker if the kids stay here with your mother. She seems to have improved since the death of your father. She treats me with respect and kindness now. She's polite. And she loves the kids unconditionally — that's a plus."

So far, his mother still doesn't know I'm Braven's original soulmate — Malisty. We decided long ago that no one else is to know about my past.

My mind flicks to Marcus. Braven's little brother. The one who came to the house after the death challenge, demanding answers, demanding blood. Braven calmed him down enough to listen to reason, and then Marcus left. No one has seen him since. His mother becomes vague whenever his name is mentioned. I can't tell if she's protecting him... or if she truly doesn't know anything.

"Yes," Braven says quietly. "Mother has changed for the better since Brian's death."

He leans down and gives me another quick kiss — one that leaves me hungry for more.

"When you get back, we'll finish round three or four."

I jut my bottom lip out in a pout.

Braven laughs, shaking his head at my antics as he jumps out of bed and heads toward the bathroom first.

Bugger.

Round three has to wait.

I release a contented sigh, watching my sexy husband disappear through the doorway. A huge smile spreads across my face as I admire the biteable, toned arse that vanishes into the bathroom.

How did I get so lucky? My heart and soul feel like they're bursting with love and joy — for Braven, for our children, for the life we've built. After the sad past I endured, after the lies, the loss, the pain... I am one lucky woman.

I found my soulmate.

I regained my memories.

I returned home.

I'm surrounded by family and friends.

And I married the man I love.

What more can a girl ask for?

Epilogue

Misty

AN HOUR LATER, I'M DRESSED, FED, AND SIPPING THE last of my sweet tea. The warmth settles in my chest, steadying me for the day ahead. I've already cuddled my babies — all three wriggling, giggling bundles of chaos — and taken another round of selfies with them. The kids love having their picture taken, especially now that I've mastered the fun photo app. Big eyes, silly ears, sparkly crowns... they squeal every time the filter pops up.

I snap a few more, kiss their soft cheeks, and send the photos straight to Braven's phone with a message reminding him — again — that he missed the kids this morning. He'll pout about it later, I'm sure. My big, muscly alpha who melts into a puddle when his cubs smile at him.

I give them one last cuddle, breathing in their warm baby scent, before grabbing my briefcase and heading toward the door.

Thank the gods for the clan — for the pack members who

stepped up without hesitation and became our instant nannies. Including Braven's mother. I still keep my guard up around her, though. She loves the children fiercely, and I know she would protect them with her life. But when it comes to me... there's something there. Something I can't quite name. A shadow behind her eyes. A hesitation in her smile. A question she never asks out loud.

Maybe she would have preferred someone else for her son's mate. Maybe she senses the truth I'm still hiding — that I'm not just Misty, but Malisty. Maybe she knows more than she lets on.

I sigh softly as I lock the door behind me.

Hopefully, one day soon, we'll become friends. Hopefully, trust will grow. Hopefully, whatever that strange feeling is... it will fade.

But for now, I tuck it away, slide into my car, and start the engine.

Time to face the city. Time to face the council. Time to be the alpha's mate, the mother of three, and the woman who somehow juggles financial reports with supernatural politics. And gods help anyone who tries to ruin my morning tea buzz.

NEARLY THREE HOURS INTO MY TRIP, I TAP THE steering wheel and decide to call LJ. If traffic keeps behaving, I'll reach the city early enough for a quick lunch before my one p.m. meeting.

"Call LJ," I say, and my car obeys.

Her voice fills the cabin by the third ring, warm and familiar, like she's sitting right beside me. "Hello, stranger."

"Why, hello, LJ. How's city life treating you?"

"Why, if it isn't Ms Kitty girl. Are you on your way to the city?"

"Yes. I should be arriving early enough for us to meet up and grab some lunch before my one o'clock meeting."

"Fantastic. Should I meet you close to where the meeting is? That way you don't have to rush off and find another parking spot."

"That sounds brilliant. I'll meet you in about an hour at Southbank. We can dine at one of the Crown restaurants. The meeting's in the Metropol conference rooms."

"What about the financial reports?"

"I had a few minutes this morning before the kids woke up and sent a copy to you. Can you handle the correspondence for me in case the meeting runs overtime?"

"Sure thing, Misty."

"Awww. Thanks, babe. I'll owe you one."

Something prickles at the back of my neck. I glance up at the rear-view mirror.

A blue car creeps closer. Too close. Shit. The idiot is practically kissing my bumper.

I flick my eyes to the speedo — I'm sitting exactly on the limit. The other lane is empty. There's no reason for anyone to be this close.

"Misty, are you still there? Hello, Misty..."

Ahh, shit. LJ.

"Hey, LJ. Sorry. I've got some idiot tailgating me, and they're getting closer."

"Hey, it's okay. You have to concentrate on the road."

"Thanks, LJ."

"Umm... Misty, whereabouts are you anyway?"

"Ah, the last sign said Pakenham. A few more to go. And yes, I'm still on the M1. Why?"

"Hmm. Just wondering. What's the car doing now?"

I check the mirror again. "Oh shit, LJ. They're about two feet off the back of my car."

"Misty, I want you to put your foot down and turn off onto one of the exit ramps. Travel along the old Princess Highway toward Melbourne. Can you do that for me?"

My pulse spikes.

I press harder on the accelerator, weaving past a few cars, eyes flicking between the road ahead and the blue menace behind me. I aim for the exit ramp and slip onto it.

I check the mirror. The blue car follows.

"LJ, I'm on the Pakenham exit ramp, and that blue car is following me. Now what?"

"Look, Misty, I have you on loudspeaker and JJ is here. I'll have him phone Braven. I'm starting to have a bad feeling about this."

"Okay, LJ. That makes two of us."

A moment later, Braven's voice bursts through the speaker — raw, sharp, panicked. JJ must have hit hands-free.

"Braven, can you hear me?" I raise my voice as the blue car closes in again.

"Misty. Baby, what is going on?"

"Braven, I was speaking to LJ, arranging lunch, when I noticed a blue car tailgating me. LJ told me to get off the M1, which I've done, but the car followed me. It's right behind me again. If I brake, they'll hit me. I'm starting to worry."

"Misty, you must remain as calm as possible, baby. We will try to get you through this."

"Braven... let the kids know I love them. Always remember, baby, I love you with all my heart and soul."

"Misty, I love you too."

The impact hits before I can breathe. "Oh shit!" I scream as the car slams into me from behind.

The impact is brutal — a violent punch that whips my body forward so hard my seatbelt bites into my chest, then snaps me back against the seat with a sickening jolt. The steering wheel jerks violently under my hands, twisting my wrists. Pain shoots up my arms.

Before I can breathe, another bang — harder — slams into me.

My head snaps forward. My teeth clack together. My vision blurs. I lose control. The world tilts.

A third hit smashes into the side of my car, a bone-deep thud that rattles my ribs. The entire vehicle lurches sideways. Tyres screech. The road disappears beneath me. The scenery outside my window smears into streaks of colour — green, grey, sky, road — all blending together.

My stomach drops as the car lifts — actually lifts — off the ground. For a split second, everything hangs suspended. Weightless. Silent. Wrong.

Then gravity grabs me by the throat. The car flips. Upside down. Sideways. Over and over. Metal screams. Glass explodes. My body slams against the seatbelt with each violent rotation.

Something hard cracks against my shoulder — my handbag,

flying free. Something else smacks my cheek — a water bottle. Loose coins scatter like bullets, pinging off the roof — now the floor — as the car rolls again.

I hear LJ and Braven shouting through the speakers, their voices warped and stretched by the chaos, like they're underwater.

My phone tears free from its cradle and flies past my head, missing me by centimetres before smashing into the passenger window.

A hiss fills the cabin — sharp, chemical, terrifying. White explodes around me. Airbags. Powder. Burning rubber. The acrid smell of something electrical frying.

The car rolls again — metal crunching, glass shattering — the roof buckling with each impact. My head whips sideways. My neck screams. My ribs feel like they're being crushed. Another roll. Another slam. Another explosion of debris. A final violent jolt slams me still.

Silence.

Except for the tinkling rain of broken glass settling around me.

I hang upside down, suspended by my seatbelt. My hair dangles toward the roof — now the floor — tangled with shards of glass, receipts, pens, the contents of my handbag, everything that wasn't bolted down.

Loose items continue to fall — my sunglasses case, a rogue baby sock, a packet of wipes — all thudding against the ceiling beneath me.

I wiggle my toes.

Nothing.

Shit.

I try again.

Still nothing. A cold wave of terror washes over me, icy and suffocating.

Stay calm, Misty. Stay focused. You're alive. That's the main thing.

The airbag droops in front of me, blocking my view of my legs. The stupid fabric clings to my face, smelling like burnt plastic and chalk. I try to push it aside, but my arms tremble violently.

Maybe the steering wheel is pinning my legs. Maybe the dashboard collapsed. Maybe the door crushed inward.

I don't know. I can't feel anything below my hips.

Blood rushes to my head, throbbing behind my eyes. My vision pulses. I tilt my head, trying to see, but pain slices through my neck and shoulder like a hot knife.

Something wet trickles down my face. I lift a trembling hand and swipe at it. Blood. Warm. Sticky. Mine. Shit.

Voices drift from outside the car — muffled, distant, distorted by the crumpled metal. My heart leaps.

"Can anyone hear me?" I shout, my voice cracking. "Help! I'm trapped in my car and bleeding! Help me!"

Panic claws at my throat, sharp and relentless.

I look toward my phone — cracked screen, half buried in my hair, tangled in broken glass — just out of reach.

I stretch my fingers toward it. Pain shoots up my arm. I gasp. I can't reach it. I can't move. I can't feel my legs. My breath comes in short, frantic bursts.

"Braven... LJ..." I choke out. "If you can still hear me... the car has crashed. I'm upside down... I can't move... I'm bleeding..."

The phone crackles faintly.

Braven's voice filters through — panicked, desperate — but I can't make out the words.

I keep repeating myself, like a mantra, like a lifeline. "I love you, Braven. I love you, Braven. I love you, Braven."

Metal shrieks. Plastic tears. The car door rips away from its hinges. Sunlight floods in, blinding and harsh.

A shadow fills the doorway. A figure leans in. I blink through the haze, trying to focus. Dark eyes. Dirty clothes. A scent I recognise.

No.

No, no, no.

It's one of the homeless men from my first day in Lakes Entrance. One of the wolves.

Panic detonates inside me. "Stay away from me!" I yell, voice raw. "I'm not going anywhere with you or your boss! You're from the wolf pack, aren't you? You're that homeless-looking guy!"

He smirks, teeth flashing. "Well, well, well. Look who I found."

His voice slithers through the wreckage, smug and satisfied. "I warned you to stay away from the cat. Did you listen? No."

A sharp sting pierces my arm. "Ow—" My gaze drops. A syringe glints in his hand. My tongue thickens instantly, my words tripping over themselves. "What... what did... you do... to... m—"

My limbs go heavy. The world tilts again, this time from the inside out. I just hope... my phone... still working...

What are you d— The thought dissolves before I can finish it.

My mouth won't form words anymore. My vision swims. My body is no longer mine.

I reach for Braven through the mind link — the last thing I can do.

'Help me, Braven.'

His answer slams into me, raw and terrified. *'Hold tight, baby. We are coming. I love you—'*

Then his presence rips away.

Silence. Cold. Empty. My heart stutters. I try to blink, but everything blurs.

The wolf's face wavers above me, distorted, melting into shadow. "Malisty," he murmurs, voice fading into a distant echo. "You silly girl. Now look at the mess you're in."

Darkness swallows me whole.

Afterword

Well... if you've made it to this point without throwing your book, your tablet, or your nearest household object — congratulations. You've officially survived the end of Book One.

If your heart is pounding, your jaw is on the floor, and you're yelling at me through your screen... or at the page — good. That means I did my job.

Misty's journey has been one hell of a ride: from rediscovering her past, to reclaiming her power, to falling in love with the mate she was always meant to have, to fighting for her life — and her cubs — more than once.

And now...

Her POV ends here, mid-kidnapping, mid-panic, mid-"oh shit".

Her world goes black.

Her mate bond cuts out.

And she has no idea what's coming next.

But Book Two?

Oh, that's where things get fun.

We jump straight into Braven's POV — right as he hears the crash, feels the link snap, and realises his mate has vanished. And trust me, you've never seen an alpha lose his mind like this man does.

Meanwhile, Misty wakes up somewhere she shouldn't be, with a life that isn't hers, and a husband who definitely isn't Braven. No memories. No answers. No way out.

Two soulmates.

Two different worlds.

One hell of a fight to get back to each other.

Thank you for sticking with me through the chaos, the claws, the magic, and the emotional trauma.

You're amazing.

And you're not ready for what comes next.

Make sure to have the box of tissues handy.

Book Two is out now.

Brace yourself — Braven, Malisty, and Xavier are done playing nice. They play to live. Read to discover what happens next in Kept in the Dark Of Lies and Deceit

~ M. L. Tompsett

BOOK TWO
LOOK OUT FOR THE NEXT INSTALMENT

Kept in the Dark of Lies and Deceit.

MALISTY

You wake up in the hospital and discover you have no memories and you're married to a sexy hunk of a man named Xavier. What would you do?

Malisty keeps having the same recurring dream of a faceless man who shouts for Misty!

Who is Misty?

With her memories starting to come back – Malisty discovers she is in love with two men. How will she pick one, or can she have both?

Will Malisty discover the truth and escape the small strange community she lives in with Xavier. Or will the wild-looking wolves which roam the community attack them first?

BRAVEN

My wife has been missing for far too long. From what information we had gathered, an unknown wolf pack had taken my wife.

A recurring dream keeps my love and hopes alive for my wife, even though my pack keeps informing me she has to be dead. I refuse to believe them, and I have faith we will find Misty soon. I know deep down she is still alive. I just want her back in my arms and with our children where she belongs.

Can Misty and Braven find their way back to one another? Will their love keep their mate bond intact?

In a fight for their lives, can Malisty and Xavier survive, or will the Rogue Wolf pack keep Malisty prisoner to create a superior shifter army?

Thank you so much for reading, **Kept in the Dark of Love and Lust**.

I am honoured you have selected this book.

I hope you enjoyed being submerged in the world of shifters with Misty and Braven.

Thank you, make sure you grab the second book and continue to enjoy the characters in the world of Misty.

I am always writing, so keep an eye out for the next book.

If you enjoyed reading this book, please consider leaving a review where you purchased it. This will help other readers make a choice to select this book and to discover a new author.

The best way to say *thank you* to your favourite author, is by leaving a review. Even if it is only a few words 'I like it, page turner' - 'I enjoyed it, couldn't put the book down'

Please visit me at:

http://www.mltompsett.com

And sign up to my newsletter, for all the latest information on the next release and competitions - giveaways.

I would love to connect with you on Facebook: https://www.facebook.com/M.L.TompsettAuthor

ACKNOWLEDGMENTS

To Reece a big *Thank You* with lots of hugs and kisses, without your assistance my book covers would only be half as good.

To my beta readers, thank you for reading the words, over and over again.

Sally, Emma, Chris, and Michele you women rock. Thank you for your reading abilities, thoughts and ideas. And a special and patient woman - Amy. Thank you.

Sally and Michele I do love you guys, and thank goodness, you put up with my arse as much as you fantastic women do. You have allowed me to bounce ideas, even confusing you at which book I am speaking of.

I appreciate all the hard extra miles you have put in.

Big hugs.

www.ingramcontent.com/pod-product-compliance
Lightning Source LLC
Chambersburg PA
CBHW031220120726
47905CB00002B/410